BROKEN PETALS

An Appalachia-Inspired

Short Story Collection

Jan-Carol
Publishing, Inc

"every story needs a book"

BROKEN PETALS

Second Edition March 2014
Mountain Girl Press
Imprint of Jan-Carol Publishing, Inc
All rights reserved
Copyright © Jan-Carol Publishing, Inc
Cover Design: Janie Jessee and Tara Sizemore
Book Design: Tara Sizemore

ISBN: 978-1-939289-32-2
Library of Congress Control Number: 2014931744

You may contact the publisher:
Jan-Carol Publishing, Inc
PO Box 701
Johnson City, TN 37605
E-mail: publisher@jancarolpublishing.com
jancarolpublishing.com

Jan-Carol Publishing, Inc,
dedicates this collection of works
to the loyal, hard-working staff.
Each one of you demonstrates the faith in
and true values of perseverance,
tenacity, and resilience.

CONTENTS

FOREWORD

At about the same time that I was starting Jan-Carol Publishing, Inc, Tammy Robinson Smith was opening doors for numerous authors and readers with the creation of Mountain Girl Press. At the time, we and our companies were unknown to each other. Nor did Tammy and I realize how our paths would cross.

When Tammy decided to sell her company in 2012, her aim was to see Mountain Girl Press continue to thrive and, by doing so, nurture and inspire its authors, fans, and loyal supporters. I am honored that Tammy felt that Jan-Carol Publishing, Inc, could realize these goals. Because of Tammy, my own dreams of publishing have reached new heights. With her encouragement and guidance, *Broken Petals* becomes the first anthology for Jan-Carol Publishing, Inc, under the imprint of Mountain Girl Press.

Many warm thanks go to Tammy, and I can only hope that she takes pride in her accomplishment in creating an entity that continues to touch many lives each day.

And even a truly heartfelt 'thank you' seems insufficient for all the authors who were willing to bear the pains of transition from Mountain Girl Press to Jan-Carol Publishing, Inc, and for all our fans, supporters, and readers who buy our books.

I hope that you enjoy *Broken Petals*, the most recent collection of short stories inspired by the influences of Appalachia.

ABBY'S SECRET

Rebecca D Elswick

Before the first blade of grass was slain in the field, Abby prepared her Florence Nightingale supplies: cardboard boxes of different heights, last winter's threadbare flannel pajamas, and a sterilized eye dropper that was her own special substitute for mother rabbit's breast. Abby was the rabbit expert in the family. Her father, who gave compliments sparingly, told people in his no-nonsense way that she had a unique ability to raise the motherless wild things. At nine years old, Abby soaked up his praise and wore the recognition like a Purple Heart.

Abby's father was a farmer. Their farm was on a big piece of land he called the Old Home Place. Abby knew the cows on their farm needed hay as food during the winter, which was why her father planted the flat bottom land with grass that grew so tall she could stand in the field and disappear from sight. Abby knew her father counted on it to fill the barn loft with bales of hay. Abby also knew, to rabbits, the flat bottoms seemed like a safe haven for building nests in the spring, but when the grass developed brown heads and reached the harvesting state, it was not the rabbits' best habitat.

Abby thought summer was like living the same hot, dusty day over and over. She woke at the same time every morning, did the same chores, and spent the rest of the day playing outside until the afternoon heat drove her indoors to the stack of comic books she kept by her bed. It wasn't until July brought miners' vacation and haying time that Abby's life changed.

It was the summer of 1955, and Abby's father said it was going to be a good haying season. The grass was tall and thick from the spring rains, and the summer had delivered less humidity than usual to the mountains of southwestern Virginia. Strong winds had not laid the top-heavy blades to the ground in a twisted, mangled heap that made it harder to cut. When Abby watched her father take the plow off the red McCormick tractor and replace it with the cutting machine, she knew the time was getting close, and she knew that her boxes were in the basement ready for the soon-to-be homeless bunnies.

Abby's father listened to the weather forecast every morning, noon, and night. While they all sounded the same to Abby, her father said he was waiting for the weatherman to get the 'percent' just right. For days, the chance of thunderstorms kept her father working in the garden instead of the hay field. Then on the third morning during the week of miners' vacation, Abby heard the old pick-up truck with the tags that said 'Farm Use' going down the hill. Abby figured if her father was going to get his brothers, then the radio weatherman had finally gotten the percent right.

When Abby heard the pick-up coming up the hill, she raced out the door and greeted Uncle Henry and Uncle Tivis with a hug. Her uncles were coal miners, and they were dressed in the same

2

dark clothes and heavy boots they wore to the mines. The knees of their pants had a metallic sheen, like the coal dust was so ground into the fabric that no amount of washing could remove it. They looked strange next to her father in his blue jeans, white t-shirt, and cowboy boots. Abby's father was tan from long days working in the fields, but her uncles were ghostly pale. Abby knew it was because they spent their days working underground in the coal mines.

Abby went back inside to help her mother with the breakfast dishes, while her uncles walked up to the barn with her father. Abby was putting the dishes back in the cabinet when the tractor started. She looked up at her mother who smiled and nodded, so Abby ran outside to see which direction the nose on the tractor pointed. She saw that it was headed for the lower south bottom.

The tractor crossed the bridge over the creek. Abby loved to play in the cold creek water that was so translucent she could see the crawdads before they could latch on to her toes. Abby knew this was the same creek that ran through the fields where the cows grazed, and she often watched them come to the creek to drink. She knew that sometimes on hot days, the cows would stand in the water, which was why her father told her never drink creek water.

Abby watched the tractor pass. Her father drove and her uncles stood on the back of the tractor, holding on with one hand. They smiled and waved at Abby, but her father stared straight ahead at the meadow. Abby knew hay cutting was serious business to her father.

Abby sat down on the edge of the field and turned her face toward the morning sun. She sat for a long time and listened to the tractor and watched the grass sway in the breeze. She wondered if the grass looked like the waves upon an ocean. Abby could not speak of oceans from personal experience, but she had heard her Aunt Helen and Uncle Sid talk about the vast body of water called the Atlantic Ocean. Aunt Helen was her mother's sister and even though they had the same blue eyes and blonde hair, Aunt Helen looked sunnier, somehow. When the sisters stood side-by-side, Abby's mother looked like a wilted version of Aunt Helen.

Every fall, her aunt and uncle would visit and enthrall Abby with tales of the salt air, blue water, and white waves that rolled into shore and left traces of ocean life in the sand. Once they brought Abby a dried seahorse as evidence that strange creatures really did live in the salty water. Abby kept the seahorse in a shoebox, and in the winter when it snowed and the cold kept her trapped indoors, she took it out and dreamed of a place called Myrtle Beach with endless miles of sand stretched out alongside an ocean as blue as the sky.

It was early afternoon when Abby heard the tractor stop. Lunch was over and the dishes were done. She knew the tractor had not stopped for a water break—it was too soon. Something unexpected had happened.

Abby put aside *The Flash* comic book she was reading for the fourth time, and ran outside. Her father was walking across the bridge with his sweat-soaked shirt rolled up over his belly to make a make-shift pouch. Abby ran to meet him, and he greeted her with a 'get your box look' that made questions unnecessary.

For the next three weeks, Abby fed those five baby rabbits cow's milk carefully poured from a brown stoneware pitcher with all the cream skimmed off and saved for butter. She warmed the milk to just the right temperature, even if it took four or five tries to get it right. When the bunnies were large enough to eat greens, she picked fresh clover and alfalfa, which proved to be their favorite. She threw in some plantain for variety, since her mother said the youngsters needed an assortment of vegetables to grow up big and strong. By the end of the second week, Abby moved them to their intermediate-size box. Five days later, they were able to jump out of the box and onto the kitchen floor.

Abby moved the rabbits into the next tallest box and, she knew, the dreaded time was close, so she avoided any situation that might lead to discussion of the need to turn the rabbits loose. It was a delicate subject, one she preferred not to address until the hurdle of the toilet paper box was reached—it being the tallest box of all, coming up to Abby's shoulder. Each morning, Abby faced the fear that today was the day, so she spent every spare minute with the young rabbits.

The dreaded day came before the rabbits had been moved to the tallest box. Abby did not agree they were big enough to survive on their own. She did not agree her Uncle Henry should turn them loose, even though he had volunteered to do so behind the house, where a long trek up the hill revealed a flat section of woods.

Abby gave the adults her most wide-eyed look, but she spoke not a word. She did not protest. It was a 'children should be seen and not heard' world, and she dared not risk the wrath that would come if she voiced a child's opinion or protested against an authoritarian figure. She dared not say that if this premature release absolutely had to be done, then she had nursed and mothered and loved; therefore, she should be the one to free them. She dared not risk the red mark that would make her ears ring for the next two days. She spoke not a word in defense of the voiceless bunnies. Instead, she simply watched Uncle Henry vanish from sight, his arms wrapped around the box in front of him.

A week later, Abby was still wandering around the yard, looking for something to do, but nothing was remotely as gratifying as mothering baby rabbits. For a while, she drew pictures in the dirt with a stick, and then she sat back and thought about the rabbits. Like a sudden streak of lightening, a grand idea occurred to her—she would go up to where Uncle Henry had released the rabbits and call for them. Surely, they would remember her voice and come to her!

Abby climbed the steep hill until it topped out into an expanse of woods. There was the box—still upright. Even though she was hot and out of breath from climbing the hill, a chill swept over her, making the hair on the back of her neck stand up. She wanted to turn around and go back the way she'd come, but she needed to look in the box—she had to look, even if sad emptiness waited there.

Six steps and Abby was at the box. She peered inside and there they lay. Five little rabbits in rigor mortis—their bodies stretched out, their eyes staring in open permanence. Abby stood in stony silence. She did not feel the sun beating down on top of her head, nor did she hear the crows arguing overhead nor the cows lowing down in the pasture. Instead, she was mesmerized by the cardboard cage of death. She wanted to run away to a time when this horrible thing had not happened, to a time when she was safe in the 'adults know everything' world. A world that had been violated.

Abby knew the rabbits were unable to escape the box. She would have released them gently, one-by-one into the Brer Rabbit underbrush. She would have sat cross-legged and watched them until they disappeared into the woods, whispering goodbye to each other. And she would have allowed herself to feel pride in what she'd done. Now, she stared down at the lifeless creatures and felt guilt replace blood in her veins. She had not voiced dissent. She was responsible for their deaths.

Abby went down the hill to the meadow where her father had discovered the bunnies. She sat down and looked out at the fields where the mown grass had already turned brown and stuck up like tufts of short hair. A few weeks ago, the grounds had been beautiful with tall swaying grass that hid a warren of baby rabbits from their sight. Abby decided she would not cry but would bury her sorrow under her guilt of not saving the bunnies. She realized it didn't matter that she could mother the homeless rabbits. What good had she done if she wasn't able to save them from the adults' cruelty?

In the days that followed, Abby kept her discovery, guilty night-mares, and grief a secret from everyone. She knew that in time, the box would be found, and the adults would protect her with their own secret while she protected them with hers. Abby never mentioned the rabbits again, but that summer was an epiphany that came too soon to a nine-year-old girl. She was never able to hide this hard-earned insight from herself, but to the adults, she was nothing more than a barefooted little girl who had a knack for raising the motherless wild things.

ALICE PEMBERTON'S ORCHARD

Lisa Hall

Ramona faced her greatest temptation each morning during her walk to work. She had to pass Alice Pemberton's place. Beside Alice's house was a fruit orchard. To a poor woman suffering through the Great Depression, those rows of peach, apple, and pear trees looked like the Garden of Eden.

It was all Ramona could do not to sneak into that field and pick some fruit. Alice would never miss it. The old widow barely stepped out of her house. All the trees were tended to by her son, James, who came by a few times a week to pick fruit and drop it into big buckets. Oh, how good one of those buckets would be for Ramona and Evan.

Evan was Ramona's ten-year-old son. For over one year, it had been just the two of them. They lived in a shack reserved for tenant farmers. Out of the goodness of their hearts, the Waddlingtons, a dear couple at their church, had allowed them to stay in the shack for free.

Ramona's bad situation was due to a combination of the Great Depression and her no-good husband. Allan had worked in construction for many years. For a time, his job was good, then the Great Depression hit, and the jobs stopped. Allan had cousins in Cincinnati. "If I go to Cincinnati, there will be some work, and I can live with my cousins for free," Allan told Ramona.

The idea of staying in Kentucky while Allan left for the city was not something Ramona minded. Their separation brought her a sense of relief. Ramona breathed easier knowing that a bunch of green mountains and a big river stood between her and a man she no longer cared to know.

Ramona had met Allan when she was just sixteen. Soon after they married, he got a job in Tennessee. Before long, Ramona had to leave Kentucky and set up house in Knoxville.

After Ramona gave birth to Evan, Allan agreed to move back to Kentucky. That way, Ramona would have her family around to help take care of the baby. It was a blessing to have her family's help, because Allan was dang sure not going to help raise his son.

Then times got financially hard. The Great Depression hit and, like so many families, they became poor. They went from being able to afford everything they needed to barely being able to finance their needs to survive.

Allan had taken pride in his ability to provide. He had never known poverty. Allan took his frustration out on Ramona.

To help with the bills, Ramona found little ways to make extra money. She sold eggs from their chickens, babysat for neighbors, and cleaned house for some of the wealthier families in town. Still, no matter what she did; Allan continued to mistreat her.

As times got more difficult, his insults increased in frequency and harshness. Instead of chipping away at Ramona's self-image, every hateful thing he said to her chipped away at the love she felt for him. Ramona could barely stand the sight of him.

Then the drinking started. While Ramona was counting change to come up with grocery money, Allan was going out to taverns. By the time he decided to leave for Cincinnati, there was no love or money left.

For the first three months, Allan was sending money from Cincinnati. Ramona was able to make the house payment and buy all of the food that she and Evan needed. Then, the money and communication stopped coming. She suspected there was another woman, but she never bothered to try and find out.

Ramona found a job at the local cannery. The job paid barely enough to buy food for her and Evan. After a few months of not making her house payment, Ramona put their home up for sale. Fortunately, the Waddlingtons offered the empty shack on their farm to Ramona.

The best thing about the tenant shack, besides that it was free, was that Ramona could walk to work. It was on those walks to work that Ramona discovered Alice Pemberton's miraculous field of fruit.

Many years ago, Alice's husband had owned a few businesses in town. After her husband's death, Alice became reclusive. She could no longer summon the strength to leave her home.

Although the Pembertons were wealthy, they had lived somewhat modestly. Their home, cars, and clothes were all adequate, but nothing fancy. Ramona always thought the Pembertons must have been good people to not flash their wealth around.

From the looks of things, they must have spent much of their time and money on fruit trees instead of fine things. Since Allan had stopped sending money, the only fruit Evan ever got came from cans. Employees got to take home cans with dents or torn labels. Sometimes Ramona would get fruit cocktail out of these defective batches. Evan would get so excited when he got to have a bowl for dessert. Ramona pretended not to like the cherries so she could give them all to Evan.

A few kids at Evan's school brought fresh fruit in their lunch pails. Evan would come home talking about who had the blueberries, pears, peaches, and cherries. Lunching on fresh fruit had become a status symbol. Ramona wondered if Evan remembered what a fresh peach or cherry tasted like.

He used to get all kinds of fresh fruit. Every time Ramona went to the market, she used to bring home the best-looking produce she could find. One time she even brought Evan a fresh coconut.

That thing was so hard. Ramona had to bust it open with a hammer. First, Evan drank the coconut milk, then Ramona shaved the fruit into thick, white curls. She could still remember Evans's little fingers grabbing those curls of coconut just as fast as he could eat them. The tips of his fingers smelled like coconut oil for days.

***

One evening in late July, Ramona came home from work to find a surprise bounty on the kitchen table. Evan was grinning from ear-to-ear. "Mama, look Mama at all this fruit!"

"Evan, where in the world did you get this?" Ramona demanded.

Tears filled Evan's eyes. "The fruit fell off the trees in Mrs. Pemberton's yard. If I didn't pick it up off the ground, it was going to rot. Somebody had to get it. It's a sin to waste food. You tell me that yourself."

"Son, you know I never meant for you to take food that isn't yours." Ramona reproached.

"I'm sorry, Mama," Evan said with tears rolling down his face. "I wanted to surprise you with all this nice fruit."

Ramona was teetering between wanting to be stern and wanting to throw her arms around her precious son. She somehow found a balance between the two.

"Evan, it's sweet that you wanted to bring me all this fruit, but we can't eat it. We have to go to Alice Pemberton and tell her what you did."

Evan fell apart. "Mama, I'm scared. What if she's mean?"

"I'll go with you," Ramona promised.

The next morning Ramona and Evan took off with all the fruit in a bag so that they could apologize and return it to Alice Pemberton.

As they walked, Ramona pondered and prayed. The pondering and praying were both about the same things. How was she going to provide for herself and Evan? They were barely getting by on a combination of Ramona's small paycheck and the kindness of others. One more bad stroke of luck, and they would be flat broke, homeless, starving. Good food was so scarce that Evan had been driven to stealing fruit from a neighbor's yard.

Once they arrived, Ramona noticed something very out of the ordinary. Alice was out of the house, in the orchard.

She and Evan tried not to stare at Alice as she walked. In her day, Alice had looked both regal and strong. She had walked with a purpose, with her back straight and her chin up. The frail, slumped-over lady was a mere shell of what Alice had been only a couple of years ago.

"Umm, Mrs. Pemberton," Ramona said as she approached Alice.

In the sweetest voice Ramona had ever heard, Alice responded, "Yes, dear."

Ramona continued, "I am so sorry to bother you, but I brought my son, Evan, here to confess something to you."

Evan began to speak. "Mrs. Pemberton, I got this fruit off the ground in your yard and took it to my mama for a surprise. It was stealing, and I was wrong to take something that wasn't mine."

Evan's voice was shaking. Ramona kept a hand on his shoulder, half-afraid her son might pass out from being so nervous.

The already pleasant look on Alice's face softened even more. "Evan, you are a sweet, brave, and honest boy to come here and apologize to me. Ramona, you are a good mother to raise such a virtuous young man. Please keep and enjoy all of the fruit in that bag."

Ramona and Evan were both relieved by Alice's kindness. They did just what Alice had requested. They sat down at the kitchen table and enjoyed nearly every bite of the fruit.

The only thing they did not eat were a few peaches that Ramona had set aside. With those, she made Alice a peach crisp. While it was still warm, she got Evan to take it up to Alice's front door.

Alice's son answered the door. "Hi, I'm Alice's neighbor, Evan. My mom made this for her," Evan said as he handed over the warm dish.

James thanked Evan and promised to give it to his mother.

A few days later, Alice's son delivered a paper sack full of fruit and a basket of blackberries. "Mother really loved her dessert you sent," James told Ramona as he handed over the bag and basket.

Ramona yelled for Evan. "Come here! Alice sent us fruit!"

She loved hearing the excited rush of Evan's footsteps running to see the bounty of Alice's surprise. There had not been many fun surprises in Evan's life for some time.

Before they fell on hard times, Ramona loved surprising her little boy with toys and trinkets. Those surprises had ended when Allan quit supporting them. It was nice to have something fun and new in the house, even if it was just fruit from a neighbor.

Evan had the sweetest way of expressing how grateful he felt for the fruit. "Mama, why don't we say a blessing before we eat some fruit. I'm so thankful for Miss Alice Pemberton!"

They held hands across the kitchen table and bowed their heads in prayer. As Evan offered up a simple, sincere prayer, Ramona silently offered up her own prayer of thanks. Despite everything that had happened, Evan was a good boy with not one smidgen of anger or resentment for what he had endured.

Ramona was not the only one who noticed what a good boy Evan had become. Over next few weeks, Alice Pemberton was made fully aware that he was an outstanding young man.

One day, after a summer storm, Evan went into Alice's yard and cleaned up tree limbs. Evan never told Alice what he had done, but she saw him through her living room window.

Another time, when it was raining really hard, Evan took Alice's mail and newspaper right up to her front door. When Alice offered Evan a dollar, he refused the pay, even though he really could have used it.

Evan kept doing small acts of kindness for Alice. In return, Alice kept sending her son up to Ramona and Evan's house with bushels of fruit to show her gratitude. In appreciation for the fruit, Ramona always sent Alice some cobbler, preserves, or some other treat made from the fruit. It became a beautiful, unending circle of kind acts and gratitude.

***

One crisp evening in November, Alice's son knocked on Ramona's door. Instead of the usually sack full of fruit, James was holding an envelope. His face looked weary and sad.

As he spoke, Ramona could tell that something was very wrong. "I'm so sorry to disturb you, but I have terrible news. My mother passed away this morning."

The announcement made Ramona cry. "Oh, I am so sorry. What little I knew of your mother, she was a kind and generous lady."

Despite his grief, James mustered up a smile. He was about to let Ramona know the extreme depth of his mother's generosity.

He handed Ramona the envelope. "Mom thought a great deal of you and Evan as well. She knew that her last days were upon her. About a week ago, mom gave me this envelope. She said to make sure you get it."

With trembling hands, Ramona opened the envelope. Inside was a note.

> *Dear Ramona:*
>
> *The kindness and integrity you and Evan demonstrated in my final days meant a great deal to me. Although I sent fruit as a token of thanks, there is something more I would like to do.*
>
> *After I am gone, maintaining my home and fruit trees will become a burden to James. He has a home of his own, children, a job, and other responsibilities.*
>
> *It is with a happy heart and James' blessing that I leave my home with all of its land to you and Evan. I am certain you and Evan will enjoy it so much. It gives me peace to know that the home where we raised our son will once again have a fine young man growing up within its walls.*
>
> *Sincerely,*
> *Alice Pemberton*

***

"Mama, it's so early. Can't I sleep a little bit more?" Evan asked.

"Evan, you know we've got lots of work to do," Ramona told him.

As Evan rolled out of bed, Ramona noticed how tall he had gotten. "Pretty soon you're not going to need a ladder to pick fruit," Ramona joked.

Once Evan's feet, hit the floor, his movements picked up speed. He quickly dressed, ate breakfast, and headed out the door.

His early morning would be spent harvesting fruit from the trees and berries from the vines. Later, he would take his harvest to the little stand he had built by the road in front of their house. While he sold fruit, Ramona would be in the kitchen, making pies, jellies, and apple butter to sell in the stand.

Before the stand opened, Evan had one more important task to complete. The new sign for their fruit stand still had to be painted. It was time to give their operation a name, and Evan had come up with the perfect one. With some strokes of the paint brush, Evan finished the sign that read "Alice Pemberton's Orchard." Under the name was a simple statement that summed up how their business began in the first place:

"Our bounty is meant to be shared!"

APPLES TO APPLES

Lori C Byington

"Sheriff! She's done it again! Mabel's stolen my apples. I can see the buckets on her back stoop! Get over here and quick," yelled Myrtle into her new Motorola cell phone. "This darn phone won't hold a charge," she said to no one but her gray cat, Blue Boy, who was lounging under an old apple tree lazily licking his right paw.

"I guess he got my message. Motorola is supposed to be a good one, but I can't prove it," Myrtle huffed as she walked back up the small hill to where her gravel driveway met her house.

Myrtle had been in the snow-white, three-bedroom, two-bath home for as long as she could remember. She still loved the Corinthian columns on the front stoop. She had won a newly married couple's argument with Tal long ago. He had wanted no columns at all. They would make the house, and them, seem pretentious, he had argued until he was blue in the face. Myrtle won the argument only because the builder had talked her husband into going with the columns instead of just a plain board fence around the front.

"It'd make the whole stoop pretty as a picture," the builder told Tal.

Tal had only nodded, and that was all Myrtle needed for an OK on the matter.

Myrtle smiled at the memory as she looked at the front of her home, which was nestled in the foothills of the Holston Mountains. Myrtle remembered vividly when she and Tal, short for Talmadge, were first married and decided to build their own home rather than buy on of those Sears and Roebuck prefabbed homes that were popular in 1930s. The only reason the new couple had been able to afford to build their home was because Tal had recently been promoted to Assistant to the Assistant Post-Master. What a blessing the promotion had been! The new job had moved them to Goodson, Virginia, which was smack-dab on the border of Tennessee. In fact, Goodson was a twin city. Half of the city was in Virginia, and the other half was in Tennessee. The split made for confusion for outsiders due to the two police departments, two school boards, and two of just about everything one could imagine. Those were great times, Myrtle thought. As she continued to admire her home she noticed the Williamsburg-blue shutters needed painting again. Painting could wait though. She had an apple-napper on her hands!

Sheriff Carmack sighed and looked for his car keys. He calmly shut his Verizon cell phone and got in his patrol car to drive to see why Myrtle was in such a tizzy.

I have to miss my lunch meeting with the fire chief at Shoney's on 'breakfast Wednesday' over some suspected stolen apples? He thought to himself. *Can't she just go to Piggly-Wiggly like everyone else for her produce?*

Begrudgingly, Sheriff realized he needed to check on Myrtle's frantic call about Mabel and apples. He did not know what Myrtle was likely to do!

Myrtle and Mabel had a long history of life in Goodson. From their childhood neighborhood to finally settling down in their own homes, the ladies were somewhat like family to each other, although they also loved to hate each other. Myrtle blamed Mabel on a pony-riding accident that apparently happened when they were both five, and Mabel blamed Myrtle for 'stealing' a prospective suitor after they graduated from high school. Neither story was true, but it made for good gossip when necessary. Myrtle and Mabel had been great friends, but time and circumstances had separated them further than either realized. During their college years they kept in contact weekly. Myrtle would venture north to Hollins College where Mabel went to school, and Mabel came home frequently because her parents were in the same town. Myrtle had chosen an in town college to attend and lived at her parents' home.

Neither thought they took their friendship for granted, but truth be told, Myrtle and Mabel were too much alike to share the same space for long. It may have been their distant blood ties or it may have been their damn stubbornness, but no matter the reason, they grew apart. It was only after Mabel's husband passed away and Myrtle's husband slowly developed dementia that they found each other again. Both were in the same predicament—loneliness—and both needed something to bring them back together as true friends. It so happened that fate, God's fruit and Myrtle's habit of jumping to conclusions helped spur the reunion.

About twenty minutes later, Sheriff's honey-brown official-looking car pulled into Myrtle's drive. He looked like a TV movie star when he stepped out of the car. He was complete with an officially issued 9-mm in his holster, but he kept his bullets in his pockets.

"One can never be too careful," he told everyone who would listen.

In reality, Sheriff was really afraid he might shoot off his foot, but he would never admit it.

Before he could say a thing, Myrtle said, in a not-too-polite voice, "I promised a pie an' apple butter to my brother, Donald. Now how am I to keep my promise with her taking my loot?"

Sheriff hiked up his pants, as he so often had to do when he stood up, snorted, and drawled out, "Slow down now, Myrtle! Let's start from the beginnin'. How do you know Mabel stole your apples?" he asked her directly.

Myrtle was squealing at this point, and her patience was gone—not that it stayed long anyway.

"Look at her back porch! It's plumb full of bushels of apples! My apples!" Myrtle steamed adamantly. As Myrtle said "apples" her voice rose two octaves, which made Sheriff grimace. *Sure glad she doesn't sing in the First Baptist Choir*, he thought to himself.

Myrtle's gray-blue eyes twinkled in the sunlight, and her unlined face did not give away her age. She stared hard at Sheriff as if to telepathically send thoughts his way. He glanced at the back of Mabel's house. Mabel's back porch was not ten feet from Myrtle's five apple trees. Proximity alone made Mabel guilty of apple-nabbin', but proving the case would be difficult. Sheriff was not likely to be ordering fingerprinting evidence on a hundred Macintosh apples, although Myrtle would have requested it if she thought it would do her any good.

"Now, Sheriff," Myrtle said as calmly as her ire would allow. "You know I don't jump to conclusions all of the time. Just some-times, but this time I know I'm in the right."

Sheriff sniffed again and glanced at Mabel's stash of rickety, tan bushel baskets. It did appear as if Mabel had helped herself to Myrtle's loot. Myrtle's apple trees were awfully bare for a hot September afternoon. There was no breeze to speak of and the sun had reached its peak of the day, which made the daylight seem all the brighter.

"Myrtle," Sheriff began to ask, "did you see Mabel pick your apples, put them in those baskets, and carry them to her porch? That's a mighty heavy load for a sixty-five year old woman to tote, don't you think?"

Myrtle had to admit Sheriff might have a legitimate point. "She could have had help, Sheriff," Myrtle responded. "She's got a son home from the Navy, an' he's tough and could've helped 'er! He'd do anythin' for his momma. He might even steal my precious apples!" Her voice rose to an annoying whine that somehow came through her nose as she answered.

Sheriff stood quiet for a minute while he pondered the possibilities. Myrtle, unfortunately, appeared to be right, but how to prove it, and better yet, how to ask Mabel without inciting a feud was a major obstacle.

The breeze began to pick up and red, gold, and bright green leaves whirled around the yard where the bare apple trees stood guard. A lone red apple fell from its perilous perch and almost hit Sheriff on the head. He glanced down at it and thought about picking it up to eat, but he decided better of it. If Myrtle saw someone get one of her apples she really would have an apoplectic fit. Blue Boy awoke when the apple thudded to the ground. He stretched and lazily sauntered, as cats are wont to do, to see what had fallen from his personal canopy.

"Well?" Myrtle finally asked. "What are you going to do?"

"I guess you need to cautiously ask Mabel if she 'borrowed' your apples," responded Sheriff.

"What?" gasped Myrtle. "Me ask? No, no! I'm not going to set foot on Mabel's property! She's liable to sue me or use it as an excuse to come back on my side of the yard," Myrtle said feverishly. "Besides," she continued, "It's your job. Did we not elect you to 'serve and protect'?"

"Well, I guess you're in a jam," offered Sheriff. "There is no proof from what I see except for the bushels of apples. To tell the truth, the apples in the baskets look nothin' like the apple that just fell off of your tree," continued Sheriff. "Look. The apples in Mabel's baskets are more yellow. Yours are more of a reddish color. Now how could that be?" asked Sheriff. A slight grin started to spread across his face but he did not let Myrtle see.

Myrtle paused a moment. She adjusted her wire frame glasses up onto her freckled nose. It didn't help her vision one bit. She had meant to get her glasses prescription changed but hadn't gotten around to it. She had to admit she didn't notice the color difference of the apples in question.

"Oh, mercy," Myrtle said under her breath. *Maybe I'm wrong on this one*, she thought to herself.

Once that thought crossed her mind, she felt prickly heat rise up her throat and up to the top of her gray-blond hair. She immediately felt ashamed. Myrtle was never wrong in her book, so this development took her by surprise.

Sheriff noticed Myrtle's dour expression. Just as he was about to ask her what she was going to do, a delivery boy from White's Produce ran around the back of Mabel's house and bounded up the back-porch stairs.

"Howdy, Sheriff, Mrs. Counts," he said as he tipped his weathered blue King College baseball cap in their direction.

"Howdy, Jamie," Sheriff said and nodded toward the young-ster. "What's you up to?" he asked.

Jamie offered timidly, "Well, Mrs. Hall ordered these bushels of apples for butter an' pies, and when I delivered them this morning I forgot to have her sign her ticket for Mr. White. He was mighty upset with me, so I had to come back to get Mrs. Hall's 'John Hancock.' Is she home?"

Myrtle cleared her throat nervously and kept her gaze toward the crimson fruit on the ground. She kicked the apple just to make it move so she could double-check its color again.

Myrtle cleared her throat again and offered, "Well, I don't rightly know if Mabel's home or not. Why don't you rap on her door to check?"

"Thanks, Mrs. Counts," Alex said smiling. His timidness had disappeared, so he knocked on the weather beaten green door at Mabel's back stoop.

Too soon for Myrtle's comfort, Mabel came to answer the door. As she opened her door, a creaking like fingernails on a blackboard came from the rusted hinges. At least that was what the sound seemed to be to Myrtle. Mabel saw the gathering of Sheriff and Myrtle before she noticed young Jamie standing on her porch.

"Well hello, neighbor, Sheriff," yelled Mabel. "Everything all right?" she asked.

"Ummm. Yes, Mabel. Just dandy," lied Myrtle, as she obviously tried to hide her chagrin and embarrassment. "Sheriff just dropped by to, uh, help me fix a problem. It's solved now," continued Myrtle.

Sheriff just grinned like the Cheshire cat from *Alice in Wonderland*.

"Jamie is here from White's for you," relayed Sheriff.

"Oh mercy!" Mabel gasped as she finally saw the youngster standing there with a creased paper in his hand. "I forgot to sign the slip for my apples didn't I?" she asked Alex.

"Y-y-yes, ma'am," Jamie stammered. "Mr. White was a bit peeved at me when I got back to the store and there was no signature," he said.

"Well, bless your heart, young'un. I'll put pen to paper right quick so you can skedaddle back to White's," Mabel said.

She signed her charge note from White's Produce and handed it back to Jamie.

"Thank you, Mrs. Hall," Jamie yelled as he ran back around to the front of Mabel's house and headed to town running as quick as his legs would carry him.

Once Jamie was gone, Mabel yelled out, "Good to see ya'll again. Don't be a stranger, Myrtle. You're just next door. When I get my apple butter done, I'll bring you some!"

Myrtle glanced at Sheriff and knew he was heartily laughing inside. He just grinned wide, tipped his hat, and walked back to his official vehicle.

"Bye, ladies. Have a nice day," he said over his shoulder.

Myrtle, face flushed, said hesitantly, "Thank you, Mabel. Can I help carry your baskets in?"

"No, thank you," responded Mabel. "I'm going to enjoy the crisp, blue autumn sky and do my peelin' on the porch. Come set a spell why don't you. We'll catch up."

Myrtle nervously smiled and walked to Mabel's porch. "Don't mind if I do, Myrtle. It's been a while," she said. "It's been a long while."

AUNT ERNESTINE'S POSITIVE THINKING

Gretchen McCroskey

We had all heaped our plates with hamburgers, hot dogs, potato salad, and baked beans when Aunt Ernestine said, "At our next cookout, we'll be having steaks instead of hamburgers if I get my sweepstakes money."

When Uncle Frank was working at Sears Roebuck in Bristol, he and Aunt Ernestine had anything they wanted. Then when Katherine came down with leukemia, Uncle Frank had to spend so much time in Charlottesville that he had to quit his job at Sears. After Katherine died, Uncle Frank decided he wanted to move to the farm. He said, "If I'm going to be poor, I'd rather be poor in the country."

Uncle Frank had been raised in town, and he didn't know much about farming. "You'll have to start small," Daddy told him. "If you have good seasons, you'll get back on your feet in no time. Then you can buy more machinery and go into it really big."

Granddaddy Glover had left the home place to Aunt Ernestine because he said, "Ernestine'll take care of the place, and she's my baby girl." He'd left Daddy 55 acres in pasture and timberland.

Mama was a little hurt that Granddaddy Glover hadn't left the homeplace to Daddy. I once heard Mama say, "I don't care if tradition does say the home place goes to the youngest child, you're the one who looked after your dad all those years. Seems mighty unfair to me. You were the one taking Mr. Glover to the doctor, and I was the one fixing his meals and washing his clothes while Ernestine was out shopping and going to the beauty parlor and on them vacations to Myrtle Beach. We've always been tied to the land. I'd never got to go on a trip if my family hadn't lived 200 miles away."

I was glad when Aunt Ernestine and Uncle Frank moved next door, but I missed Katherine. She was my favorite cousin and the closest to my age. The week after the funeral, I lay awake at night crying because I was afraid I'd die too. One time I told Aunt Ernestine about hearing a tree fall in the woods and that I was afraid it might be a sign I was going to die. Aunt Ernestine said, "Nellie, you're not even sick. Why are you thinking about dying? Poor little Katherine was sick. I miss her so much that sometimes I think I can't stand it, but I saw her suffer up there in Charlottesville till it was almost a relief when the Lord took her. Now, don't you worry about dying. You just get busy living."

It was hard for Aunt Ernestine to get used to farm life again. And she missed all the money Uncle Frank used to bring in. Aunt Ernestine knew what it felt like to wear thirty-dollar silk blouses and shop at places like Maxine's Style Shop and The Robin's Nest in Abingdon. And when Katherine was living, she had all them fancy dresses from the Nettie Lee Boy and Girl Shop. She always looked so pretty with her thick black hair tied up in fancy gros-grain ribbon bows and wearing frilly store-bought dresses. But I can't say I ever envied her, because I loved the pretty dresses Mama made for me out of Dan River cloth that Aunt Eva, Mama's sister, mailed us from the Dan River Cotton Mill where Aunt Eva worked.

Mama and me shopped mostly at Parks Belk, Penney's, and the Dollar Store. I couldn't imagine Aunt Ernestine buying her underwear at Lowe's Dollar Store like Mama and me did. I had seen them fancy matched sets—bra, slip, and panties—in ecru, navy, and white. Mama used to stop in front of the store window at Hal Bandell's Ladies' Shop and study the silk suits displayed there. Sometimes she'd go home and cut out a pattern in the style of one of the suits and sew it herself. Mama was talented that way, but I knew she would love to march into Hal Bandell's and try on every suit in her size and then buy one without even looking at the price tag, just like Aunt Ernestine used to do before Katherine got sick.

"It's hard to come down," Mama would say. "But it's no disgrace to be poor. I think Frank is satisfied out here on the farm. But I don't know about Ernestine. She's had a lot on her, losing her daddy and Katherine and her home in Bristol."

"Well," Daddy said, "Dad had lived his life, but it's hard to give up that sweet little Katherine. Mary, I don't understand why the Lord wants to give you a child and then turn around and take it from you. They'll never get over that. But they ought to live good out here. They better be thankful that Dad left them the home place. I'll tell you, there's a whole lot of people that don't have it half as good. I'm just glad I have a little land to raise us something to eat."

"Ernestine always has been bad to spend," Mama said. "She never looked out for a rainy day. I bet she won't do all that shopping now."

Aunt Ernestine might have had to give up things, but she didn't give up her dreams. She had decided to try her luck with Sweepstakes. It was my eleventh birthday, and Aunt Ernestine had planned the cookout to celebrate. I was sitting on the old metal glider that had been on Granddaddy Glover's front porch for as long as I could remember. Topsy, my old gray cat, was stretched out beside me, sound asleep. Every once in a while, she would swat a fly off her nose, but she paid no attention to the sweet smell of charcoal and roasting hot dogs. Mama and Daddy and me always roasted our hot dogs over an open fire in the rock grate where Mama made apple butter, but Uncle Frank was grilling hamburgers and hot dogs on a little portable charcoal grill.

I sank my teeth into the juicy hamburger and could hardly believe there was a hamburger this good. Even the hamburgers that my older sisters bought me on Saturdays when we went to Bristol Drug did not compare with this. I was sitting there wishing Katherine was here to celebrate with me. If she had lived, she would have been thirteen next week. I almost didn't hear Mama say, "I threw my sweepstakes letter in the trash. I get tired of all that junk mail."

"I mailed mine yesterday," said Aunt Ernestine. "I ain't got nothing to lose but a four-cent stamp."

Uncle Frank leaned back in his rocking chair and lit a Camel cigarette. "You're just wasting your time sending in them things, Ernestine. They don't even give that money away."

"Now, Frank, all this is official. Listen to this letter," Aunt Ernestine said as she rummaged through a stack of mail beside the phone. "It says, 'Fifty lucky customers are holding entry forms just like yours that are worth $10,000 each. But only one of them—the first one to get a lucky entry to us—wins.' Only fifty people—that's pretty good odds."

"Ernestine, don't you have sense enough to know that there are probably 50,000 people who got that same letter. Paper will lay there and let you write anything on it. They probably don't give away any money at all. They just want to sell their old magazines."

Mama rallied to Aunt Ernestine's defense. "Frank, don't you remember that my Uncle Jim's son up in Ohio won $5000 a few years ago. That's more money than we'll ever make raising a tobacco crop. Why that's more money than Doris Grubb made teaching school last year and her with all that education. I believe her daddy said she made $250 a month for ten months. I'm telling you, Ernestine, I wouldn't know what to do with $10,000 if I did win it."

"I've always gone to church and tried to live right," Aunt Ernestine said. "This may be the way the Lord's going to bless me."

"Well, don't expect the Lord to bless you in gambling," Uncle Frank said. "That's gambling just as much as it would be for me to go and play a game of poker."

"No, it's not," said Aunt Ernestine. "Preacher Wilson says as long as you don't have to pay any money to enter a contest, it's not gambling."

"You women!" Uncle Frank laughed. "Just believe anything. There's nothing free in this world. The only people that have money are the ones that work for it and the ones that inherit it. Looks like I'm going to have to work for mine."

That was the end of the sweepstakes argument until one Saturday night when Uncle Frank and Aunt Ernestine came over to play rook. "Mary," Aunt Ernestine said to Mama, "I've been reading that book *The Power of Positive Thinking* by Norman Vincent Peale. He says if you want something to happen you have to believe it will happen. I've started making a list of what I'm going to do with that $10,000 if I get it."

"Frank, I bet she's going to buy you a new truck," said Daddy, who'd been concentrating so much on the game that I was surprised he'd heard Aunt Ernestine.

"No, Nathan, I'm going to give my tithe, which will be $1,000, to the church, and I'm going to send some money to Billy Graham. Trula Thompson sent him $50 last year, and she gets that *Decision* magazine. She's been using it for devotions at the circle meeting, and it has some good reading in it. I need to buy a marker for Katherine's grave. And I want to have some work done on the house. I can fix it up like those pictures in *Better Homes and Gardens* magazine."

"Frank, you better watch out," said Daddy. "Ernestine will really have you working around that old house when she gets her money."

"I'm not going to be sharpening my tools," said Uncle Frank, "until I see the check," he said with a wink at Mama.

"If you don't have faith, you'll never have nothing," said Aunt Ernestine.

That devilish little grin played around Uncle Frank's mouth, and I knew he was getting ready to tell a joke. "I'm kinda like the old woman who prayed for the mountain to be moved. The next morning she got up, looked out the window, and said, 'Just as I expected.'" Everyone laughed, including Aunt Ernestine. I didn't really catch it, but I was trying to read *Little Women*. Sometimes it was hard to decide which was more interesting—the Marsh family or Mama, Daddy, Uncle Frank, and Aunt Ernestine.

I hoped Aunt Ernestine would get the sweepstakes money because she was always giving me things. One time when she and Uncle Frank and Katherine went to Florida, she bought me a seashell doll. I just knew she'd buy me something really nice.

Aunt Ernestine watched the mailbox like I sat by the radio hoping Eddie Hartsock would dedicate a song to me. But she hadn't gotten any notice and the giveaway day, August 1, was creeping up. One day when I was visiting, Uncle Frank looked at the junk mail on the kitchen table and laughed, "Ernestine, is this your sweepstake check?" he asked.

"You won't be laughing when the mailman delivers my check," Aunt Ernestine said. But by July 29, I think Aunt Ernestine had about given up on getting rich from the sweepstakes. I saw her go to the mailbox and sift through the mail that day, and I could tell by the way she was walking back to the house that she wasn't her usual positive self.

"I think I'll walk over to Aunt Ernestine's," I called to Mama.

"Now, don't you go getting in her way," Mama said.

Aunt Ernestine was sitting on the front porch looking through a JCPenney's sale paper. "See any bargains?" I asked.

"Nothing I really need," said Aunt Ernestine.

"Don't look like you're going to get your sweepstakes money, does it?" I said.

"Not this time," Aunt Ernestine said, without looking up. "Nellie, when you grow up, find you a rich man, so you won't have it hard like your mama and me."

Aunt Ernestine and I watched *Another World* and *Days of Our Lives* until Uncle Frank came in and interrupted us. He was all excited. He came over and put his arm on Aunt Ernestine's shoulder and said, "Honey, you may get rich after all. I was up at Joe Mongle's store today, and some men from Commonwealth Gas Company came in talking about gas leases. They're trying to lease all this land around here to drill gas wells. They have already struck gas in Lee County. They've offered my cousin Henry Fields $5000 to drill on his place." I sat up on the edge of the couch, my ears fine-tuned for more. I never was so surprised as when Aunt Ernestine answered.

"They'll never set foot on this place if I have to sign any papers. I don't want them bringing in that heavy machinery and tearing up this land. Daddy said to me before he died, 'Ernestine, I'm giving you and Frank the home place because I know you'll take care of it.' I've heard what the coal companies have done over in Dickinson County. No, I'll never sign any papers to let them outsiders promise me a lot of money and then tear up this farm."

I expected them to get in a big argument, but Uncle Frank just turned and walked out toward the barn. A few days later, I heard him and Daddy talking.

"Frank, have you leased your farm to the gas company yet?" Daddy asked.

"No, they haven't contacted me," Uncle Frank said.

"They talked to Mary and me yesterday, but I want to check with a lawyer before I sign anything," Daddy said.

Uncle Frank laughed, "I don't need a lawyer. I've got Ernestine. She's dead set against it. Your dad knew what he was doing when he made out his will. He has somebody who'll look after his land."

AUNT TRISH'S WEDDING GIFT

Janie Dempsey Watts

I saved Aunt Trish's gift for last. Like my aunt, her gift was the heaviest, the loudest, and could not be ignored. For my last birthday, she had given me a jar filled with June bugs, and her anniversary gift to my parents was a garden hose, which reminded her of the couple, she said. Not the kinky kind.

"Come on, Sally!" she ordered. She was wearing a brightly flowered tunic and what appeared to be purple, polka-dotted flannel pajama pants, an outfit that looked like it was left over either from her most recent Caribbean cruise or last night's slumber party.

With some apprehension, I rose from my chair and walked to the bulky gift, wrapped in lime-green tissue and placed smack dab in the middle of the ring of chairs where my guests were seated.

"And this one, as you may have guessed, is from my Aunt Trish," I said as I read the gift card which was covered with faux white fur. "Shagadellic, baby! A special gift for you and John. Love, Aunt Trish. Thank you, Aunt Trish." I ripped off the tissue on the top revealing a giant white bowl of sorts. "Oh, it's white...it's a—"

"Feeding dish for a Great Dane?" someone shouted out. Everyone laughed. I rushed to pull off the rest of the paper, only to see a toilet bowl. Everyone laughed. I wasn't sure what to say.

"Oh, my. How original. Thank you, Aunt Trish. I think the apartment already has toilets," I said, "but we can keep it as a spare."

"You silly gal," Aunt Trish said. "Look there in the bottom." I bent down over the toilet bowl, and with some hesitation, put my hand down into the canal, a place I'd only explored before with a toilet brush. Everyone clapped and cheered me on. My fingers felt a rectangular packet. I pulled it up. A packet of zucchini seeds. Everyone laughed. Aunt Trish continued, "You can plant them seeds and see what comes up, if you know what I mean." She cackled and snorted. I blushed.

"All right, I'll do that, Trish. Thank you. Anyone want some more quiche? What about another sweet tea, anyone?" No one answered. They had all stood up and were taking cellphone photos of the toilet and Aunt Trish.

My sister motioned me over. "Sally, get over here so we can get a shot of you with our aunt and the—" she laughed as she tried to finish her sentence.

"Zucchinis," another friend shouted out. "Her zucchinis."

"John's zucchinis," someone else offered. Everyone howled except me. I had tried to plan a classy event, but Aunt Trish had, once again, taken over with her outlandishness. Mama had insisted I had to invite her. Ever the good sport, I walked over and grabbed the packet of seeds and held it up to the camera while kneeling next to the toilet.

"Me and my zucchinis, folks." I smiled while everyone snapped. Aunt Trish stood next to me, beaming. I was saved by Mama calling from the dining room.

"The chocolate lava cakes are done. And coffee." My friends abandoned the photo session and followed Mama and the smell of chocolate and coffee. I was about to walk away too, but Aunt Trish reached out for my arm and stopped me.

"I've got some potting soil in the car," she said. "Now don't you let me forget it. You can plant them when you get home from the honeymoon. If things don't work out, you'll still have John's zucchinis." She laughed at her own joke. I just shook my head and walked away to join the others. I didn't want to tell her what I really thought—she was full of it. And herself.

After the shower fiasco, I made Mama personally promise to have someone babysit my aunt during the entire wedding. To her credit, Mama kept Aunt Trish on a tight leash. Mama told Trish that she needed help watching one of our cousins who had been convicted of shoplifting. "Your job is to follow her around and make sure she keeps out of everyone's handbags." Given a task, Aunt Trish knew how to follow through. She talked cousin Millie's ear off because, as everyone knew, Trish could talk the ears off a brass billy goat. Millie didn't have a moment to spare she was so busy answering all of Trish's questions. What color was that hair dye? How much did she pay for those shoes? Where did she buy her dress? What kind of face cream did she use? Had the change affected her love life? And most importantly, who did her spraying for termites?

After our honeymoon, John and I arrived at our two-bedroom apartment and were surprised to find the toilet on our patio filled with dirt and apparently with seeds already planted. Aunt Trish had attached a note to the toilet bowl said, "Water three times a week—with water, not the other, John." John laughed. I did not.

A couple of weeks later, the seedlings had come in. Begrudgingly I watered them, not so much because I cared, but because I couldn't stand to see them die. John and I would sit on the porch and drink a glass of wine after work, and I'd glance over at the plants which seemed to be growing without much tending.

One night, we invited another couple over for drinks before we all went out to dinner. John's co-worker, Sophia, and her scruffy-looking boyfriend, Richard, were halfway through a second glass of Pinot Grigio when we wandered onto the patio. She pointed to the toilet bowl.

"Oh, Sally," she said. "A potty. How cute." Then she turned to John, "I thought you said your wife was sophisticated."

"Sally is, but her aunt isn't," John said. "She gave us the toilet. She's as large as a hippo and the black sheep of the family." Sophia reached out and touched John's arm with her svelte fingers.

"How can she be a hippo and a sheep?" she asked. "Sometimes you say the silliest things. Like last week at Franco's when you told the waiter it was our anniversary so we'd get the free tiramisu."

John laughed, and added, "That's not the way I remember it." He glanced over at me. I mouthed the words "free tiramisu?" John shrugged and picked up the wine bottle to pour her another glass of wine.

After a dinner where Sophia flirted nonstop with John, making the rest of us uncomfortable, it was time to say goodbye. When the valet brought their car up, Sophia wobbled over to John and gripped him in a long embrace. When she finally let him go, she turned to me and waved her slim tentacles, "Bye, bye hippo girl." Not looking at each other, we climbed into our car to head home.

"Why did you call my aunt a hippo?" I asked. He shifted into second.

"She is rather large, in case you haven't noticed."

"And when did you and Sophia go to lunch?" I asked. He sighed.

"Last week, and she was the one who told the waiter it was our anniversary."

"Did you tell the waiter you were married to someone else?"

"I let it pass. It was a joke. Are you going to get all jealous on me now? You go out to lunch all the time with your co-workers."

"They are women, and a few men. And none of them, not a one, ever said they were married to me, even as a joke."

"Well, the women wouldn't, that's for sure."

"What? Are you trying to change the subject here? "

"So what if I am? You're acting insecure, Sally. We went to lunch, it's not like I slept with her." He whipped the car around a corner, and I shifted in my seat.

"Whoa. Could you slow down a bit?"

"You want to drive?" He slammed on the brakes, handed me the key and jumped out of the car. "Because I don't want to be with you right now." As I watched him walk away, I sat there for a moment trying to figure out what was going on. Apparently a lot.

Back at home, I arrived to an empty house. He had not made it home and hadn't called. I walked onto the patio and looked out toward the street. No sign of him, even though it was after midnight. I looked down at the toilet bowl and kicked at it with the point of my heel before going in to undress. I hated Aunt Trish's wedding gift, I despised Sophia, and I was puzzled by John's behavior.

After a few fitful hours of waiting to see if he had come home, I stirred just before dawn to the sound of a key in the lock. I jumped up and peeked through a crack in the door. With his shirt tail out and his hair tousled, John entered the living room and headed for the kitchen. He turned on the faucet and got a glass of water before going to lie down on the couch. At least he was safe. I fell asleep.

When I awoke around nine the next morning, he was already gone. I saw a note on the kitchen counter.

The note said, "You're no fun anymore. I'll be staying at my brother's tonight." I walked out to the patio and sat down in the lawn chair next to those stubborn zucchini plants raising their leafy heads toward the new day. I read John's words again. So I was "no fun?" I looked at the toilet and thought of Aunt Trish.

Despite her rough edges, even she had a sense of humor. She had enjoyed a long and happy marriage with her husband until he passed on. I thought of Uncle Joe and his talking fish he brought to every family reunion, the way Aunt Trish always threw her head back and laughed at his same old gags as though they were new every time. Maybe Aunt Trish was wiser than I thought.

After work, I stopped off at a little costume shop a few blocks away to try on some outfits. I found the perfect one, considering the situation. I signed the rental agreement, gave the clerk my credit card, and left the store wearing my costume. Trying to parallel park wearing an animal head was hard, but I did it. Somewhat awkwardly, I walked up the flight of stairs to John's brother's place. I knocked on the door and waited. After a minute or so, the door opened. It was my husband.

His mouth dropped open when he saw me—a pink hippo standing at the door. Through the mask I spoke. I know my words must have sounded muffled. "I forgot to bring the tiramisu."

"Sally?"

"It's me. I'm ready to have some fun." He reached out and plucked the huge mask off my head and set it aside. He laughed.

"I was a jackass, wasn't I?"

I nodded. "At least you weren't a hippo," I said. He reached out and wrapped his arms around my pink furry shoulders.

"This costume is all wrong," he said. "You're more of a fox." He kissed me on my cheek.

"Let's go home," he said, taking my hand. "I hate being away from you." He held my paw and we headed to the car. He opened the passenger door and I climbed in. He handed me my tail and went back to retrieve my head.

Back at home, when I was about to take off my hippo costume, John came over and whispered in my ear, "Maybe you should leave it on, you beast."

"You think?" I laughed. He responded by squeezing my pink furry tail.

FRIED OKRA

Pam Keaton

Cheryl smiled warmly at the children gathered a few yards from where she worked. Only the day before, those same boys and girls talked and laughed together comfortably as they stepped from the school bus. Now they stood blanketed in the silence of unfamiliarity that each new morning brought. From their nervous, darting glances, Cheryl could tell the children had seen her in the garden. They seemed uncertain of how to behave in her presence. She was, after all, an adult and a stranger.

Cheryl's bare feet were covered with dew-soaked grass, but the bright morning sun cast a welcomed warmth across her face and promised a pleasant spring day. Her thin, sleeveless dress was a faded floral print with a tear in the waist seam. There were newer clothes hanging in Cheryl's closet, but she had never been ashamed to wear an old frock. She imagined it was because, unlike her grandmother, that wasn't all Cheryl had.

Stepping onto the concrete blocks of her raised garden bed, Cheryl plucked green beans from vines that had thoroughly attached themselves to a braided string trellis. As she did so, her mind went back to a time when she used to help in the garden behind Grandma's little cottage. She thought of her grandmother's rotund body in a faded, loose-hanging dress. Her skin was very tan with a few dark freckles, and her thin, graying, waist-length hair was pulled back in its customary bun. In Cheryl's memory, Grandma was surrounded by buckets and bean plants as she bent over to pick what she always called a 'mess o' beans.' Then the two of them broke beans and removed strings while, beside them, Mason jars of ice water dripped condensation and promised sporadic relief from the heat and the doldrums.

A creaking front porch chair gave Cheryl a front row seat from which to soak in Grandma's pleasant spirit; and it seemed there was plenty to spare. If Grandma wasn't speaking cheerily with passing neighbors or welcoming the occasional curious hummingbird or squirrel, she was singing gospel songs or praising the Lord for the glorious weather.

Cheryl dropped a few beans into her bucket and smiled when she remembered Grandma's singing. If Grandma ever had a beautiful singing voice, then it was gone by the time Cheryl heard it. When Grandma sang, her voice was deep and manly, but Grandma didn't seem to care. She just bounced her knees dramatically and belted it out. But then, maybe that was mainly for Cheryl's amusement.

Cheryl guessed *colorful* was a good word to describe Grandma, or perhaps *satisfied*. Cheryl never knew her grandfather because he died before Cheryl was born, but she heard that he was often abusive. Cheryl found it hard to imagine Grandma living with a man like that. It must have been hard on her—so hard that she never went looking for another man the rest of her life. Grandma never seemed unhappy to Cheryl though. Her little four-room cottage was awash with color and life. While the home Cheryl grew up in was always bare and drab with very few pictures or decorations of any kind, Grandma's house had pictures, knick-knacks, candles, doilies, colorful curtains, blooming plants and lots of books. For whatever reason, Cheryl's own mother seemed to have no hobbies, interests, particular skills, or vibrancy of personality, but Grandma had it all.

Cheryl and her siblings loved going to Grandma's house, because there they found warmth and joy. Even their parents, who often quarreled at home, laughed and talked while they all sat around Grandma's kitchen table. Cheryl guessed it was harder to be hateful on a full stomach and so soon after holding hands in prayer.

Money was tight for them all back then, but Grandma knew just what to pick up at the corner grocery and tote home in her little two-wheeled cart. When she added fresh vegetables from her garden, she had prepared something that would "make your tongue slap your brains out." At least, Cheryl thought, that was what Grandma used to say. Chicken and dumplings, deliciously salty green beans, sweet coleslaw, and buttery cornbread never failed to put smiles on the faces around Grandma's table. She didn't mind if someone reached for seconds, either, though, she did often warn that their "eyes might be bigger than their stomachs."

One time Grandma noticed Cheryl dropping another large helping of mashed potatoes onto her plate.

"My lands! Cheryl's gonna have to let out the top button of her britches, if she keeps that up," Grandma exclaimed. As the family snickered, Cheryl lifted her shirt to give her belly a satisfied pat. When she did, the whole family saw what Cheryl had forgotten. The top button of her britches had already popped off some time earlier—either in the wash or when she was shimmying up some tree or other. Cheryl's belly wasn't big, but it still pushed the loose flap open for all at the table to see, which caused a laugh from everyone—especially Grandma. Cheryl always liked the way Grandma laughed, because her laugh wasn't a small stream of dainty bubbles escaping from behind a hanky. When Grandma laughed, her big belly jiggled, and she threw her head way back, blowing out a howl that Cheryl thought might raise the roof.

Grandma always found a reason to laugh—even when she had to sell her little house and live in a nursing home because her diabetes got bad. Whenever Cheryl's family went to visit, and Grandma saw them coming in the front door, she raised her hands above her head as though she had won a million dollars. "Here comes my kids!" she squealed and then wrapped them all in bear hugs and laughed while she 'stole some sugar.'

Sadly, by the time Cheryl was twenty years old, Grandma was gone. Cheryl's siblings were married, their parents were divorced, and Cheryl was attending community college with dreams of leaving behind their sleepy little Appalachian town. Cheryl loved her family and was not ashamed of her roots, but she wanted more for the future. She didn't dream of super stardom. Still, it seemed like she ought to be able to have a different kind of life than the poverty they all knew.

By the time Cheryl was thirty, she was happily married to Ray, who shared her dream of making something happen for the two of them. Extreme wealth was not necessary, but it sure would be nice for their parents back home to have something to brag about at the barber shop, the deli counter, or the church social. Neither Cheryl nor Ray were above working hard, and they had not expected overnight success. Still, all the 'irons in the fire' never got hot enough to set the world ablaze. The bills were mounting, the collectors were calling, and she and Ray were consumed with the cares of life.

By the time forty rolled around, the economy was bad, companies were closing, real-estate values were plummeting, and Cheryl and Ray were bankrupt. The only good thing was knowing they were not the only ones whose dreams had fallen apart. That didn't make it feel a lot better, though.

Cheryl never thought of herself as a proud person, but when the job that Ray was able to find meant moving back to her hometown, she was filled with dread. She didn't want to move back there, because that would be like going backward. In that town, Cheryl and her family used to be on welfare. In that town, the police department had domestic disturbance reports listing her parents' names. In that town, some people probably thought Cheryl's dreams meant she had been trying to get 'too big for her britches.'

What were people going to think about Cheryl if she moved back home? They would probably wave and smile and ask about her mama, because it would be rude not to. But when she passed by, they would probably lean and whisper to each other, "Yep—too big for her britches."

Something changed in Cheryl when she and Ray moved back to that Appalachian town. It had to do with the way the telephone didn't ring every few minutes with some business problem to solve and the way traffic didn't drown out the birds singing or the noisiness of crickets or the occasional hooting of an owl. It had to do with how the neighbor across the street mowed his yard religiously and clipped his shrubs into 'high and tights' that would do a Marine barber proud. It had to do with the smell of smoking grills and the clinking of horseshoes hitting their mark as the older African-American gentlemen across the alley razzed each other about how "that shot was the cake and this next one's gonna be the icing."

Finally, it had to do with the way the leaves and the blooms came out on the catalpa tree and made Cheryl think the mass of rocks, saplings, and weeds beneath that tree would be an attractive planting bed with a little work. In short, it had to do—not with business or money—but with life.

Early one morning, before the sun came up, Cheryl got dressed and slipped into the cool, dewy air. While Ray slept, Cheryl leaned on the back porch post and studied the mass of briars and weeds enveloping the catalpa tree. She felt as though, for months, she been in a raft, floating aimlessly out to sea. Rowing ferociously had not gotten her to shore, but somewhere along the way she had dropped the oars and had lain back, defeated and hopeless.

That morning, Cheryl's hands itched to make something happen. So, armed with tree-trimming snips, a scythe, a shovel, and a handsaw, she attacked that small grove with a vengeance. By the time Ray ventured outside to see what she was up to, Cheryl had cut down and dragged off numerous milkweed plants, cockle-burs, thorn bushes, and locust saplings. Ray was surprised by her progress and amazed by the pile of liberated rocks and the amount of soil-encrusted garbage accumulating in the nearby trash can. Mostly, though, he was inspired.

By the time the sun set that evening, Cheryl and Ray were hot, tired, dirty, bruised, and aching, but they sat together in their back-yard swing surveying their accomplishments with satisfied smiles. The planting bed beneath the catalpa tree was lined with creek rock and was ready for whatever greenery or shade-loving flowers Cheryl might choose. Just as she had imagined, it was beautiful.

Ray had spent his day in the middle of the yard, building raised-bed vegetable gardens. For years they had talked about growing their own vegetables, but it had never seemed like they could spare the time or the energy. That year Cheryl did not make her usual objections, so Ray made it happen.

From the first morning Cheryl ambled through the gardens and bent to see new plants pushing through the soil, she was hooked. How had she forgotten the peacefulness and beauty of wit-nessing God's daily reminders of life in the world He had created?

She remembered hearing a saying about being closer to God in a garden than anyplace else, and she could feel the truth in those words. No matter what else happened in the future, Cheryl would remember that along with each new morning, week, month, and season came new possibilities.

Each year since, the garden behind Ray's and Cheryl's house grew, as did their collection of canning jars, and *How To* books. They were behind the other town residents in their knowledge of sowing, reaping, and storing up; but they were up to the challenge and they enjoyed it. Sure, they could run down to the Kroger store and pick up a jar of pizza sauce or a bag of frozen vegetables for a buck each, but it was heartwarming to experience and see first-hand how a small seed with a little watch-care would grow. God's blessing was still what sustaining life was all about.

Cheryl felt a new kinship with her neighbors and with women from ages past who turned dandelions into jelly, rhubarb into pie, and something as slimy and uninviting as okra into a fried delicacy. In fact, it was on the day Cheryl brought a skirt-tail full of okra into her kitchen and dropped it onto the table that she had an overwhelming feeling of having come full circle. As kids, she and her sisters helped Grandma pick okra, but they were so disinterested in the stuff, they never stood around to watch how it was cooked. How were they to know that one day they would enjoy the taste of it?

Standing there looking down at the dark green fuzzy pods, Cheryl realized she had no idea what actions of hers would turn those strange-looking slime syringes into the small chunks of meal-covered delight found in the frozen foods aisle. She smiled with wonder. At the time, she hadn't thought of it in that way, but it could be said that she'd spent many years trying to be *more* than what her grandmother was. Now, there she was wishing she had Grandma to call upon so she could learn a thing a thing or two from her.

With thousands of recipes at her disposal, Cheryl soon became an old hand at frying okra. She couldn't help feeling, however, that it was not the same as having learned from Grandma. As she looked out her kitchen window one day, Cheryl wondered why she hadn't realized before how close she and Ray had settled to her Grandma's little cottage. In fact, if it had not been for the trees in between, Cheryl would be able to see her Grandma's little cottage from her own front porch. *Well, my lands!*

Cheryl's thoughts returned to the present as a jogger passed by.

"That's a good-looking garden!" the jogger called as she waved. Cheryl recognized the local librarian, and she raised her hand in return.

"Thank you," she answered. "Have a good day. It looks like it's going to be beautiful!"

The librarian disappeared around the corner, and Cheryl returned to her examination of each plant's progress. As she worked, she noticed how the children at the bus stop continued stealing glances in her direction. *Children could be so curious*, she thought—*much like hummingbirds or squirrels.*

When she moved to the next raised bed and began studying her okra plants, Cheryl smiled and thought of her grandmother yet again. Then she decided to take a page out of Grandma's life book. Why shouldn't Cheryl let a few local children think of her as *colorful* or perhaps *satisfied*?

"Hey, there!" she called to the children as she pulled a pod from the plant and headed in their direction. "Have any of you kids ever seen okra?"

FRONT-PORCH SWING

Rachel Burdine

Annie took a deep breath, one last look around, squared her shoulders, and slammed the door before the memories that flooded her mind had a chance to drown her. It would be the very last time that she would shut the door to the house that she had called home for the last seven years.

The past year had been filled with 'last times.' The last time she would have his favorite dinner waiting on the table, the last time he would kiss the top of her head and call her Baby, and the last time she would feel that giddy feeling in her stomach when she heard his key unlock the door at the end of the day.

This year also held the first times that had rocked her world. The first time she washed lipstick that wasn't hers out of his shirt collar, the first time she found a wadded up receipt in his pocket for flowers she hadn't gotten, and the first time she was nauseated at the smell of an expensive perfume that wasn't hers when she fastened the seatbelt in his car. And finally, the very first and last time she would ever wear a long-sleeved shirt in July to cover the bruises he'd left behind when she'd mistakenly confronted him on the night he'd had a few too many.

Annie squinted in the bright mid-day sun, transferred the last box of her things to her other hip, and hurried to her now full SUV, hoping to avoid a conversation with any neighbors that might be outside. Over the years, she had grown to love the older couples on either side of her, but today wasn't a day for idle chit-chat or explanations. She wanted to get out before that familiar car turned into the driveway.

She and Andrew had been separated for the past six months trying to work things out, but neither had spoken the word 'divorce.' They hadn't spoken at all since the night a week ago when she had asked about his girlfriend. She knew without a doubt that he wanted out of this marriage, and she also knew what was holding him back—the fear of having to share his wealth, which was worth far more to him than she. What had attracted him to her in the first place she would never understand. Practical, level-headed, and frugal almost to a fault were words that would describe Annie, so far from the blue-blood type he had dated before her—and obviously during their marriage. She would give a mint to see the look on his face when he opened the door and realized she had moved out, that she was done. Settling herself behind the driver's seat and turning the key brought immediate heartache as the familiar chorus of 'their' song filled every square inch of the car's leather interior. With mach speed, Annie silenced the Bose sound system and let loose a string of expletives that would cause her mother to pray and her grandmother to laugh.

Oh, what she wouldn't give to be able to sit and talk about this hot mess with her Gran. Even though she'd been gone for over nine years, Caroline still missed her dearly, as well as her no non-sense, practical advice. Gran had been through the fire, so to speak. Raising five children and working shift work at the cotton mill while her no-good, drunk of a husband who skirted his way around town had refined her in a manner that no debutante could ever rival or understand. Gran had put up with the loser's wildcat ways until he turned an angry hand on her, and then—she was done. She always had her head held high and her Mary Kay lipstick applied, and in Annie's mind she was the epitome of a true Southern Woman. Southern in a Baptist sort of way, always blessing someone's heart, or having sweet tea on hand, or speaking sugary sweet to others, or having a casserole at a grieving widow's door before the undertaker pulled out of the driveway, but a never let 'em see you cry about your past, sweat about your situation, or fret about what you're gonna do next, kind of Southern.

Pulling into her parent's pear tree-lined driveway, Annie couldn't help but smile as her four year old son, Wyatt, came flying across the yard to greet her. "Hey Momma, I've missed you! Did you teach the boys and girls a lot today?"

"I missed you too, Wildman! I didn't go to school today, Buddy. I had some other things to take care of, and Mrs. Parker pretended to be me today. Now, were you good for Gigi today?"

Wyatt thought for a minute and said in his Southern drawl, "Yeah, I was. She'll tell you I weren't if you ask her, but I was. Well, I better go hit some golf balls, Mom." Annie watched Wyatt whack a golf ball seventy-five yards, straight as an arrow— pretty good for a little lefty. He could be a golf phenomenon if he stuck with it. It was in his blood.

Opening the storm door, Annie stepped into her mom's kitchen and shivered slightly as the cool air hit her hot skin. Seeking and finding her favorite diet drink hidden in the back of the fridge, Annie popped the tab and sank onto the nearest barstool in the open farmhouse-style kitchen. "How'd it go today,

Babe?" Annie heard her mom ask as she came down the stairs carrying a basket of laundry.

She felt the familiar pang of guilt for inconveniencing her parents by moving herself and Wyatt in with them and wrecking havoc on the comfortable routine that they had settled into during their retirement years. "I guess it went about as well as any train wreck could go," Annie said and grinned bravely taking a long slow drink. She didn't realize how exhausted she was until that confession. Whether physical or mental, this day had taken its toll on her.

"You know what I read the other day," Annie knew that coming from her mom this wasn't really a question, but a segue into something she probably wasn't in the mood for hearing, "that diet drinks cause belly bloat. That might be what's causing yours."

"I'll have to think about that mom, thanks." Annie shot her mom a wink and headed out on the porch to watch Wyatt hit.

As Annie lay in bed that night, her mind played over all the events of her life in the past two years. Was this something she should have seen coming? What choices had she made to bring her here to this place in her life? What would she do now? How would she manage raising a high-spirited little boy on her own? How would Wyatt fair in all of this? Would he be okay?

Sleep proving to be elusive, Annie got out of bed and went downstairs to get a drink to bloat her belly. The light of the full moon drew her out on the front porch, just as it had so many times in the past. There was something about the moon that had always mystified Annie. Settling on the front-porch swing, her mind wandered to all the things that the porch swing would tell if it could talk, and then counted her blessings that it couldn't.

Nights spent snuggled up under a quilt with her high-school boyfriend, promising each other the world, laughter filled conversations with her mom over a shared bag of gummy bears while they listened to the Saturday night call-in show on the local country radio station, break-ups and make-ups, one last conversation with her dad before her wedding, where she had felt Wyatt move for the first time while she swung, and finally the dawning realization a few weeks ago when she admitted to herself that her marriage was over.

All of those things played into and made her the woman she had become. But who was that woman? She certainly wasn't the love struck teenager nor was she the light-hearted twenty-year-old eating gummy bears. She would never again be the young single woman trying to make her way in the dating world, she was no longer disillusioned by the romanticism of marriage or the idea of perfect children. She was no longer the woman who could lie to herself about the condition of her marriage. But what had she learned from all those things—who was she?

Annie thought of all these things as the familiar sway of the swing provided a sense of comfort and security that enabled her to delve deeper into herself. She had learned something very important from each of these experiences although, she didn't realize it until this very moment. She had experienced sweet, innocent love. She had learned to laugh without abandon. She had learned what she wanted in a partner and what she didn't. She had learned that her dad cared for her immensely even though he had always had a difficult time showing it. She had felt life inside her and learned what it was like to love someone with all your heart before you even met them. She had also learned that there is a tremendous amount of strength that comes with being honest with yourself. The hard part about knowing all these things was figuring out which person you wanted to be, or maybe the real you was a culmination of all those 'yous' of the past and the people who touched your life.

Annie had to admit that she had a lot of her Gran's spunk, but she also carried her mom's serving heart and sometimes her dad's tendency to be reserved. And maybe it was all a choice.

Maybe by deciding how you wanted to react in a situation made you the person that you became. Maybe there could be great joy in deciding for yourself who you wanted to be and how you wanted to react to life. Annie had no idea how long she sat in the swing, piecing it all together like the patchwork quilts made by her Gran, but she did know that the sun was making its way above the familiar line of trees and the peacocks at the farm down the road had started talking to each other for the day when she made her way up the stairs and crawled back into bed, and finally sleep came.

The next morning Annie awoke to a gentle pat on her face, a smile in her heart, and peace like a river in her soul. Opening one eye, her heart melted as she met the gaze of the sweetest thing she'd ever known. "Good morning, Mama. You want to snuggle?"

After twenty minutes of The War of the Tickle Monster, the pair decided it was time to head downstairs. Annie's dad met them at the bottom of the stairs. "Hey, Berry," her dad called her by the nickname she had since she was little, "we're going down to the Farmer's Market. You guys want to go with us?"

Annie caught a glimpse of herself in the mirror hanging over the mantle and didn't know whether to laugh or cry. Her auburn hair was piled on top of her head in what only could be described as a "wad." Too many nights without sleep had resulted in making her look like she was akin to a raccoon, and her mismatched pajamas consisted of Hello Kitty sleep pants and a Rod Run t-shirt. Going out would require way too much effort and quite possibly a wand. "No, Dad, I guess not. I promised Wyatt a Monster Truck Rally here in the living room. You guys go ahead."

Upon hearing the sacred words 'Monster Truck,' Wyatt slid sideways into the living room looking like he'd just participated in a cock fight and lost. Half of his hair was standing at attention and the other half looked like it had surrendered to the North. "Excuse me, did someone say, 'Monster Trucks?' Yeah, man! We are ready!"

Thirty minutes later, after Wyatt had insisted on a breakfast of Spaghetti Os, half of which were on his face. The two sat cross-legged in the floor as their favorite band's latest CD provided the music for the makeshift Monster Jam. They were quite a sight, the two of them. Annie smiled to herself. Just then the doorbell rang and Annie peeped out the side window to see two Jehovah's Witnesses standing at the front door. "Oh crap! Just what I need!" Annie snapped as she went to open the door.

Before she could even greet the unwelcome intruders, Wyatt was at her side, crossing his arms, and leaning against the door-frame. "Well, hello there, Crap! My Momma says you're just what she needs!"

At that second, Annie heard the band blare in the back-ground, "Tell the grave digger that he better dig two—dig two!"

The mortified man looked at Annie like a deer caught in head-lights and said, "Perhaps this is a bad time. We'll just leave this information and pray for you. Turning on his heel he headed to his car faster than a scalded dog, followed closely by his accomplice.

Still shocked by the entire incident, Annie shut the door and looked down at Wyatt's grinning tomato-sauce-stained face. She didn't know whether to laugh or cry—but decided to laugh. Annie threw back her head and laughed. She laughed until her sides hurt and tears streamed down her face. She laughed until Wyatt joined in, although he had no idea what was so funny. She laughed until she almost couldn't stop. She laughed without abandon, like a twenty-year-old eating gummy bears. And when she was finished laughing, she scooped up her sweet son into a big hug and felt his Spaghetti Os kisses on her cheek.

At that very moment, Annie knew one thing without a shadow of a doubt: Wyatt was going to be fine—and so was she.

HALLELUJAH HOMECOMING

April Hensley

The wide foyer of the little white country church was backed up with people as they all tried to enter at once, quickly becoming a lively social gathering spot. Excited greetings rang out and sincere welcomes were expressed as, from inside the sanctuary, a lone soprano sang a beautiful heartfelt hymn a cappella. The mournful wail of Jimmy Collins's blue-tick hunting hound Toby accompanied the singer, though no one seemed to notice. Katie Lynn Moore's head was spinning with the names and faces of the large amount of humans and their furry friends she had greeted in the last hour. With minutes to spare before worship began, Katie Lynn slipped discreetly out the doors for a much needed moment of solitude.

The tall covered concrete porch of St. James United Methodist Church was empty, but it wouldn't last long. Taking a deep calming breath, the fair-haired twenty-nine-year-old smoothed her neat pixie cut with her slender hands and straightened her ankle-length white robe. The young woman glided over to the black metal railing, which was just out of reach of the late-morning September sun. Standing there so still and confident, she could have been a queen surveying her kingdom. On closer inspection, though, one would see gentle blue eyes gazing serenely from a makeup-free face and an impish upturn to her lips, hinting at mischief.

Below and to the left of Katie Lynn was the cemetery, separated from the church by a line of young maple trees. It was dotted with granite memorials to those who had lived and loved in Silver Springs, Kentucky, for over 150 years. Many graves were decorated with artificial flower bouquets, but the cheery buttercups, friendly Johnny-Jump-Ups and the occasional fuzzy dandelion dotting the bluegrass gave the area a bright and inviting atmosphere. To her right was the white boxy fellowship hall. Picnic tables had been set up around it. The tasty aroma of fried chicken and freshly baked bread wafted out the door as people came and went, dropping off homemade dishes for the homecoming dinner. Her belly growled loudly. She'd been too nervous this morning to eat. In front of her, down the long flight of brick steps, was the gravel parking lot. Most Sundays it was close to empty, but today folks were driving around looking for a spot and double parking. No one would know by looking at the full parking lot that the church was in danger of being closed down due to low attendance.

Heels sounded on the steps, and she knew her brief respite was over. Stepping forward she saw it was Dorothy, a dedicated regular member of the church. Dorothy had made her feel right at home three months ago when she moved here from Virginia to begin her new assignment in the Appalachian Mountains of Kentucky. Dorothy's no-nonsense attitude, salt-and-pepper hair and merry chocolate brown eyes reminded Katie Lynn of her beloved late grandmother.

"Pastor Moore!" Dorothy smiled warmly as she steadily climbed the steps with the aid of her glossy oak cane. Under her other arm was Layla, her pink beribboned Yorkie.

"How are you on this fine day?" Dorothy hugged her firmly and quickly. Katie Lynn greeted Layla with a gentle rub on her silky head. Keeping her arm around the younger woman's shoulders, Dorothy turned so they were looking the same way.

"Well, my dear, it looks like the idea of yours to have an old-fashioned homecoming worked." Dorothy swept her arm to include the parking lot, the fellowship hall and the church as a whole. "Today is going to be a huge success, and the weather couldn't be more perfect."

"Oh no, without you I would have never thought of it. And it would never have happened without all the hard work y'all did."

"Actually, my suggestion was 'desperate times call for desperate measures.'" They grinned broadly at each other.

One night on the phone, new pastor Katie Lynn had confided to Dorothy the church would be closed at the end of the year if attendance didn't improve. The church board had informed her of this before she had accepted the position as pastor. The adventurous woman loved a challenge and wanted the job even more. Dorothy had mentioned the idea to have a homecoming. Labor Day weekend had been chosen for the event.

On a normal week, only six members attended. Pastor Moore and the 'Super Six,' as she liked to call them. The six regulars, which were two men and four women (one of whom was Dorothy), had contacted all current members, friends, neighbors, friends of neighbors, and anyone else they could think of to invite. Two months later, they had over a dozen musical talents, a full house, and what looked like enough vittles to feed an army.

Normally docile Layla gave a sharp bark and growled low at something in the parking lot, causing the pastor to jump. Dorothy gave Katie Lynn's arm an encouraging squeeze and headed inside the church. Pastor Moore heard loud yelping and looked over the railing towards the cemetery.

"Now that was my idea," Katie Lynn mumbled ruefully. Ole Hallelujah Herman, one of the Super Six, was trying to tie his horse Bella's reins to a tree. Everyone called him by the loving nickname because he would burst out a loud "Hallelujah!" without warning. Widow Brown, another of the Super Six, walked primly by him carrying her Chihuahua, which wore a purple sweater and barked nonstop. Katie Lynn was glad Herman hadn't tried to bring his horse inside. Her composure slipped, and she giggled into her hand before her brow furrowed. The only members of the animal kingdom that she had ever adopted were goldfish. She wasn't prepared for how noisy and active all the furry visitors already were. She hoped she didn't come to regret her idea of the flock bringing their four-legged friends.

The ambitious pastor got the idea for people to bring their pets to church when she had visited several senior citizens. A lot lived alone and their furry family was closer to them than children. She'd also read and watched on television that pets were good for alleviating stress and therapy for children. After much prayer she'd told everyone they would be welcome to bring their animal family for the homecoming as long as they were safe to be around and under control.

Pastor Katie Lynn straightened her shoulders, sent up a quick prayer, and stepped into the foyer. Fidgety eleven-year-old Christopher was peaking around the door, anxious to ring the bell. She signaled to him with a nod of her head. He rushed over to pull the rope hanging out of the ceiling, calling everyone to worship. Residents of the town had told her the tolling bells could be heard over the whole valley.

The choir and the congregation stood to sing the opening hymn *Lead Me Gently Home, Father*. There was a festive feel to the air. The unison of voices praising God echoed from the vaulted ceiling, causing the Godly woman's heart to swell with joy. On the way up the center aisle, she greeted friendly parishioners on both sides and was introduced to more pets, mostly dogs, a few cats, and one tiny cockatiel. There was a gamey scent in the sanctuary mixed with the clean smell of perfumes and colognes.

The self-possessed pastor reached the front and climbed up to the pulpit. The choir finished up the final words of the hymn while Katie Lynn looked out over the crowd. From this angle, she could see the church was packed full. To her, the gathering looked like a beautiful field of wildflowers with all the colors of the rainbow swaying and moving with the music. Fears of the many different types of critters being in the same place were alleviated. The creatures seemed soothed by the music, except for Charlie who hadn't stopped yipping yet and Toby, still howling along with the music, much to the amusement of the teenage crowd sitting in the far back row. As the song tapered off, Katie Lynn motioned for everyone to be seated.

"Good morning and welcome! Thank you all very much for coming out. We are going to have a wonderful, spirit-filled, blessed day. You might have noticed the singing began at 10 this morning, and lots of talented musicians will continue to entertain us throughout the day." Katie had to speak louder to talk over some of the canines starting to occasionally bark with Charlie. "We are having an old-fashioned homecoming with a twist. We decided it would be great for everyone who was interested to bring their precious pets with them. Of course we are all God's creatures. It just made sense to include our furry loved ones on this special day of fellowship." The pastor proceeded with the regular church business of asking for prayer requests and talking about needs in the community.

"We are only going to be spending about thirty minutes on the sermon this morning, then we will get back to the singing and the most important thing on everyone's minds—the food." Katie Lynn beamed brightly. Herman sitting on the left hollered out, "Hallelujah!" causing several chuckles.

"We are going to be reading from Matthew 22, verses 33-40. We will be talking about what God means by loving your neighbor as you love yourself and what to do when the person makes it hard to love them."

Katie Lynn began to read from the Bible looking up occasionally. Toward the end of verse 38, her eyes captured a trio of animals. Numbly she realized she couldn't remember the name of the dark, middle-aged man with the yellow-headed cockatiel. He was sitting about halfway back on the aisle. His chirping little bird kept flitting between his shoulder and his hand. Across the aisle and one pew back, red-haired preschooler Rose gently stroked her Maine Coon kitten on her lap. Rose and Princess both had the same big green curious eyes. Princess was using hers to watch the bird while her fluffy tail switched back and forth rapidly. In the meantime, Widow Brown was sitting with Charlie three pews behind the gentleman with the bird. Charlie's barking had grown more agitated as his focus was solely on Princess.

The pastor's voice trailed off as she watched the situation unfold seemingly in slow motion, but happening in only seconds. Like clockwork, the bird landed on its owner's shoulder, but this time it moved to the arm of the pew. That's when Princess pounced into the aisle and Charlie bolted away from Widow Brown and charged the cat with sharp barks, which set off all the dogs in the church. There were loud cries of "Princess!", "Charlie!" and "Cracker!" An audible gasp was emitted from almost everyone in the church, including the pastor, as folks jumped up, twisting and turning to see what was happening. When Charlie reached the feline, Princess calmly fell on her side and smacked him soundly on top of the head. Charlie instantly went silent and lay down docilely beside the cat. Cracker had successfully escaped back to his master's shoulder.

Pastor Moore was paralyzed. Both hands clinched the pulpit. Animal parents were anxiously trying to calm their pets, while Widow Brown and Rose were in the aisle retrieving their disobedient furry loved ones. Most everyone was still standing, murmuring to each other and still trying to see what was going on. It seemed they had forgotten all about her and Sunday service. She admitted dejectedly to herself the whole day, maybe more was ruined, and it was her fault. On the plus side, at least Charlie had finally quit barking.

Suddenly the comedy of the scene before her really hit her, and she burst out laughing. The group as a whole swiveled around in unison, and silence filled the whole church. Wide eyes were now on her and mouths hung open while Katie stood mortified with her hand over her mouth, but still shaking with laughter. That's when she snorted. The whole sanctuary roared with laughter. Katie Lynn chuckled along, unashamed. As the merriment slowed down, someone in the crowd piped up an idea.

"Maybe today's sermon should have been about the lion and the lamb!"

"Hallelujah!" Herman shouted out, and then the hilarity started again.

The amused woman of faith wiped her tears of glee away and got started on the lesson again, while everybody visibly relaxed and settled down. The animals stayed calm and quiet, too, their guardians keeping a closer eye on them. Several ladies snuck quietly out near the end to start getting the foodstuffs set out. She finished up the message with an impromptu reading of Isaiah 11:6.

"In that day, the wolf and the lamb will live together; the leopard will lie down with the baby goat. The calf and the yearling will be safe with the lion, and a little child will lead them all." After prayer, Pastor Katie Lynn Moore closed her Bible with a warm smile to the crowd. "Thank you all so much. Let's all go enjoy the wonderful food and fellowship." The choir finished up with *All Creatures of Our God and King.*

Pastor Moore received many smiles, hugs, and hearty handshakes long after the service. Now she quietly watched from the porch again. Young people congregated with jokes and overloaded plates on the church steps. Children raced by with snatched cookies, while picnic tables filled up quickly. An overweight black lab trotted by with a roll gripped tightly in her jaws. Music and song rang out from the open doors of the church. A long line of individuals snaked out from the fellowship hall, patiently waiting their turn to dive into the chow.

As she walked up to get in line, Farmer Sullivan's wife Margie handed her a Styrofoam plate filled with boneless friend chicken, old-fashioned pea salad, two deviled eggs, and a homemade roll. Several people hollered for her to come sit with them when she heard first-grader Billy Rogers talking to his grandpa in a loud, excited voice.

"Boy, this is the most fun I've ever had!"

"Amen!" A dozen more agreements rang out in the crowd.

"Hallelujah!" Ole Herman was eating with Widow Brown and Charlie by his horse Bella on the cool grass.

"Hallelujah," Pastor Katie Lynn whispered with a smile and a silent prayer of thanks.

HOLDING PATTERN

Lynda A Holmes

"I thought I was going nowhere.
Now I can see there was a pattern."

—Kate DiCamillo

I chewed with a vengeance on my sugary gum, smacking it in a manner so obnoxious that Dad ordered me to "stop that noise in the back seat." I kept chewing but closed my mouth, hoping my ears would quit popping due to the increase in elevation as we drove up the side of Lookout Mountain. Great-Aunt Myra lived on the mountain, and we were on our way to visit her for the first time in my life. I was eleven years old in that summer of 1962.

I looked forward to meeting 'Aunt My,' although I was a bit skeptical of what a mountain woman would say and do. Her reputation was that of a no-nonsense, tough person with little regard for anyone who tended toward whining or complaining. She knew family stories that Dad said were "half truth and half question mark" involving our paternal ancestors.

Mama and Dad planned a day trip to see Aunt My and enjoy the beauty of the mountain and the Appalachian countryside. Although I had been to Rock City and tourist attractions like Lookout Mountain, I had never visited anyone who actually *lived* on the mountain. Born in Atlanta, Georgia, I only knew about life in the city and its suburbs, except for the occasional visits to the rural countryside when we visited my maternal grandparents' farm.

"Dad, will we be able to understand what Aunt My says to us?" I asked.

"Of course," Dad replied, and I could see him shaking his head at my question while he kept his eyes on the road and hands on the steering wheel. I watched his body language from my vantage point in the back seat of our Buick as he continued, "She speaks English, the same as we do."

Mama turned to look at me from the front seat. "Myra is a great lady, and she is glad to have us visit her. She invited us, in the first place."

I had more questions. "If she lives all alone and has no car or truck or phone, how does she get her groceries?"

Mama smiled, glancing at Dad and answering my question. "Well, I think she keeps a garden, and she has friends and relatives who pick up her other groceries and bring them to her. She sews quilts and crafts for her friends and family, and they help her out whenever she needs anything."

Dad told Mama and me about nearby Chickamauga National Park and Cemetery and how the Rebel Confederates held off the

Union soldiers for a brief but shining moment in the War of Northern Aggression, back in 1863.

"No doubt, Myra will be showing us her piece-work and sharing story connections," Dad said, "so show respect for her and behave yourself."

Mama added, "I think Aunt My is kind of a celebrity around here."

We climbed up, up the side of the glorious mountain in our Buick on an equally glorious day of sunshine and clearest, blue skies. A small, gray house set off by an empty clothesline and the neatest garden one ever laid eyes on greeted us as Dad slowed down, parking the Buick. A non-frightening scarecrow presided over the garden. He wore clothes full of patchwork in bright colors and an old straw hat.

Fresh mountain air filled our nostrils as we got out of the Buick. Before we could get to the front door to knock our presence, an energetic, elderly lady with eyes a-sparkle burst through the doorway and began hugging each one of us. Myra smelled of Ivory soap. She wore a long-sleeved, checkered blouse and an ankle-length skirt that swished against my legs. Her salt and pepper hair was pulled back into a bun on the back of her head.

I thought I was watching all of us acting out parts in a movie.

"You must be Iris," Myra said, looking straight into my young eyes. Although she appeared delicate and her skin was wrinkled; I sensed underlying strength. Aunt My would have to be strong physically and in character to survive way up here on the mountain—without transportation or telephone. She knew we were coming because of letters sent back and forth between her and Mama. Dad and Mama would repair and paint some furniture for Myra, and we would receive her blackberry jam and crafts in return.

Aunt Myra paused a few seconds, studying me in such intensity that I wondered if I had already done something wrong, and I didn't even know it. I looked at Dad and Mama.

Myra smiled and commented, "Iris will write our stories—mark my words." I knew better than to ask a question at that point. How did Aunt My possibly know what I would do?

The answer came later.

We stepped into the perfect house. Everything was spotless ,and there was no clutter, whatsoever. Mama was strict at home about cleanliness and keeping things in order, but Myra was the all-time Queen of Clean. I had never seen such a place except in a museum. Dust was nowhere.

The kitchen curtains were lacy and whiter than sweet milk. A silvery pump stood beside the sink for Aunt My to retrieve water from her well. Cushions made from colorful, quilt squares lined the back of the sofa and every chair. There were footstools here and there, covered with fabric that matched the sofa pillows. Yes, Aunt Myra's handiwork announced her talent, loud and clear.

Old people in framed, black-and-white photographs stared back at me from the walls around the room.

Aunt Myra invited us to sit down. I gently touched the footstool closest to me, thinking it was too pretty to dare placing my feet on it, with or without shoes. Aunt My described how she made the stools from large, empty soup or juice cans that she bound together with cord and covered with batting and fabrics fashioned into her favorite quilt patterns.

"That's the *Hands All Around* pattern," Myra said. "It reminds me of everyone holding hands together in a circle as my family did, saying grace before meals. I had five siblings, and your Dad's father was one of them. He would tease me because we were so close in age, the two youngest children."

Myra introduced us to herself and her family members in the photos. While Mama and Dad got to work fixing up the kitchen chairs, we heard stories about Myra's sister, Great-Aunt Maisy. She and Myra used to dress alike and wear their hair the same style because they resembled one another as much as identical twins. Actually, Maisy was two years older than Myra. They posed as each other occasionally, and no one could tell them apart. Neither girl married. Maisy and Myra both lived on Lookout Mountain until Maisy died in her sleep a few years ago.

In one of the photos, Aunt Myra looked about my age. She wore a long dress and a necklace with something dangling from it.

"That's a fairy stone," Aunt Myra explained when she saw me studying the photo. "My Granny gave it to me. Her Mama received it as a family heirloom passed down for generations. People believed that fairy crosses would protect those who wore them, particularly those who had the Sight."

Myra continued, "Granny inherited the Sight. On the night after the Battle of Chickamauga, Granny 'saw' Grandpa in her mind's eye, lying prone on the ground. He clutched his chest where his Bible protected him from the shots that brought him down while he defended the Confederacy. If not for the Good Book, Grandpa would have died right away. Because of Granny's ability, the family was able to find Grandpa and revive him. Otherwise, they would never have found him in time. He lived for several more years, after that. So many ladies walked that battlefield, searching for their loved ones. So many families lost their soldiers that very night."

I wondered if Dad would call this story "part question mark." I certainly believed it. While I thought about life and death hanging in the balance during the Battle of Chickamauga and what it must have been like to have the Sight, Myra handed me a cornhusk doll wrapped in a mini-quilt and a tiny chair. I thanked her, and she described how she created the chair from a milk carton. Myra showed me how to find a spot for storing special items inside the chair by raising the cushion. She had cut, sewn, and stuffed fabric over and around the milk carton, as an upholsterer would do for a grown-up chair.

Myra invited me to look at her bedroom. A grand *Tulip* quilt covered the bed, which was way up high compared to my bed at home. A stepladder waited next to it, for a boost up there. I thought beds that high off the ground existed only in fairy tales. I imagined myself as a princess in a castle when Aunt My said I could climb up on the bed. I named my cornhusk doll Irene, so we could be Iris and Irene, two real princesses instead of one in our versions of *The Princess and the Pea*. We acted out our stories time after time, while Myra went to help Mama and Dad.

Later, all of us admired the freshly painted kitchen chairs as we ate slices of Aunt Myra's blackberry cordial cake and drank lemonade.

When Aunt My left the room to write down her cake recipe, I whispered,

"Mama, I need to go to the restroom."

Mama said, "No, you don't."

"Yes, I do," I replied. "It's an emergency."

Mama led me to the front door and opened it. She pointed to a little shack on the side of the front yard. "There's the restroom."

I scampered through the doorway and out to the shack, thinking that it was a shame for Myra to walk outside to use her bathroom. It wasn't until I opened the door of the shack and saw the wooden planks with spaces between them and magazines stacked here and there, that I realized this was an outhouse. Shock swatted me in the face, and I stood there, unable to move. I had read about houses with no inside facilities but had never seen an outhouse first-hand.

The outhouse was completely opposite of everything else about Myra. How could that pristine lady go to the bathroom out here, with the flies and bugs and who knew what else?

It was at that moment I had my epiphany: Myra did not consider the outhouse a hardship. It was all in one's perspective—we must do the best we can with what we have and persevere through it. Aunt My was a classic example of resilience.

An unmistakable stench mixed with the summer heat made me nauseous.

I stumbled toward the back of the privy and gagged repeatedly. Then, I turned and walked back to the house. I knew that I would stay in a holding pattern until we got back down the mountain to a regular bathroom. I would make it, without an accident and no whining or complaining.

Mama whispered to me, "Did you go?" and I answered, "No. I'll wait."

Myra appeared with more gifts for us to take home with us—a homemade quilt and some jars of blackberry jam. Though still dazed from the outhouse experience, I noticed the *Hands All Around* pattern on the quilt. The same design in each square was hand-stitched in fabric scraps of plaids, pastels, polka dots, and other colorations. It was gorgeous.

Irene and I waved goodbye to Aunt My and the scarecrow from the back windshield of the Buick. Settling down in my seat, I lifted the cushion of the tiny chair. There, in the secret compartment was a fairy stone with a necklace. It must be the one that Myra wore in her childhood photograph—the same one that had been passed down through the family for generations.

I picked it up, studying its design, the reddish-brown color, and texture. Having no children, Aunt Myra had chosen me as the recipient of this cherished, family heirloom. Instantly, it dawned on me that Aunt My also inherited the Sight. She *knew* that some day I would write our family stories, because of her ability.

I knew that Myra's prediction was truth—not question mark. Our heritage was like the *Hands All Around* pattern, holding onto me through family, culture, and lore.

Some day I would write our history—one story at a time.

I WILL CRUSH YOU

Linda Hudson Hoagland

Crushing the can, he looked up at me and said, "See, Ellen, just like this can. That's what I want to do to you the next time you open your mouth about wanting a divorce."

I backed away from him. His eyes were telling me that he meant what he was saying.

"Edward, we don't love each other anymore. We're no good for each other. All we do is argue," I said, defending myself against his threat.

"You heard me, Ellen. I will crush you," he hissed angrily.

I said no more.

Telling him the truth wasn't going to work. I had to catch him with one of his ladies. I had to force him to let me leave. It had to be something he did wrong. If he caught me doing something he didn't approve of, he would kill me, in the same way he crushed that can.

I waited until he called me and told me he was going to have to work late. He knew I couldn't check on him because he had the car. He knew I couldn't get a girlfriend to drive me around because he made sure he discouraged anyone who even tried to be my friend.

How was I going to follow him?

Anyway possible: by bus, by cab, or on foot. One way or another, I would catch him with one of his ladies.

The bus system would run its routes until nine. It was only six now. I could get to the other side of town without any problem.

I was sure he would stay away from my side of town because of the recognition factor, not so much that I would see him, but that our neighbors would.

I quickly changed from comfortable sweats into a good pair of jeans, a t-shirt, and my tennis shoes so that I would blend in with the crowd.

My nerves were jangling, but I kept my mind focused on the task at hand, which was to catch Edward with one of his ladies.

"You can be replaced, Ellen. Anyone off the street can replace you," he screamed at me during one of our many loud exchanges of ugly, bitter words.

"You go right ahead and replace me, Edward. But keep in mind, if you do, I will make it permanent," I screamed back in hurtful anger.

One of those replacements—I needed to catch him with one of those replacements. I needed to do it soon before our verbal battles carried us into physical battles. I knew I would be on the losing end if it became physical.

I ran to the bus stop and waited for its arrival. My world seemed to be filled with moments of 'hurry up but wait.' It was almost six-thirty before the bus appeared, and I climbed aboard with determination.

"Driver, do you go to Jefferson and Adams Streets?"

"Yes, ma'am."

"Would you yell it out when you get there? I'm not sure where it is."

"Sure, okay, but it will be a while," said the polite bus driver.

I sat in the seat directly behind the driver and watched the structures of my small town pass me by like they were the ones moving, not me in this bus.

"Am I doing the right thing?" I asked myself, knowing full well that my answer was "Yes, without a doubt I was doing what was totally necessary."

"Jefferson and Adams, next stop," shouted the kind bus driver.

I stood up next to the driver and thanked him for his assistance. When the bus ground to a halt, I exited and stood on the sidewalk looking around for familiar words printed on a sign. I wanted to start from Edward's workplace and walk to the nearest drinking establishment.

Todd's Camera Shop was a tiny little storefront wedged into a space between Dollar General and Subway.

"There's the car," I whispered loudly as I looked around to see if I could find the happy philanderer.

I didn't see him, but I saw a noisy bar with flashing neon lights and a fanning front door as people entered and left the establishment. That was the kind of place he was attracted to. It would definitely be his home away from home.

I fluffed my hair, pulling it down to cover part of my face so I wouldn't be so easily recognized, then I straightened my backbone and walked into the bar like I had done this everyday. It was barroom, dark inside with little lights that were equivalent to nightlights shining from various areas of the room. The darkness made it difficult to see faces clearly. You had to almost be standing next to people to be able to recognize them.

I walked around the room looking for friends with whom to sit. At least, that was what I wanted any onlooker to believe.

After my second trip around the room, I took a detour into the ladies room. I let a few minutes pass before re-entering the noisy bar. I glanced around again and didn't see Edward. I was so disappointed, and at the same time I was relieved.

I exited the dark bar and stood on the sidewalk again, trying to figure out where to go. His, I mean *our*, car was still parked on the street, and he was nowhere to be seen.

I saw a motel sign flashing in the distance. Maybe he and one of his ladies got themselves a room for the evening.

I walked to the camera shop where I stood in front of it, peering inside to see if I could see him wandering around in there after hours. Unless he was hiding in an unlit backroom, I could not see him at all.

I pulled my set of car keys from my jeans pocket and climbed into the car. I would drive to the motel. I didn't feel comfortable walking down the darkening street for such a long distance. Anyone or anything could come out from between the structures and do me harm.

"Has Edward Sklarz registered here?" I asked the desk clerk.

"Take a look for yourself. I don't recognize the name," he said as he turned the room register toward me.

I didn't see his name or his handwriting, if he was using an alias.

"Thanks," I said with a great deal of disappointment as I turned to leave.

"What should I do now?" I asked only myself. "Should I just take the car and go on home and let him know that I was checking up on him? Should I park it where I found it and find a way home just as I had planned to do?"

To save myself from bodily harm, I knew what I had to do. I parked the car where I found it and started walking to find a bus stop. It was only about eight-thirty, and I still should be able to catch a bus headed for home.

Finding the undeniable reason to get rid of Edward did not work as I had planned. It would someday. Of that, I had no doubt.

About an hour later, I walked through my front door to an empty house. I was so glad he hadn't made it home before I had.

I was starved, so I made dinner for the both of us. I wolfed my portion down ravenously and placed his in the microwave for him to reheat when he finally arrived.

I walked to our bedroom and fell into bed, an exhausted and disappointed wife.

I awoke during the night to a pounding at my door. I glanced at the clock, and it was around two-thirty in the wee morning hours. I was startled and confused.

I threw on my robe and ran down the hallway mumbling, "He's going to wake the neighborhood."

I unlocked the door and jerked it open expecting Edward to be leaning against the door in a drunken stupor.

What I saw were two policemen.

"Are you Ellen Sklarz?" asked one of the policemen.

"Yes," I answered in a barely audible tone.

"Is Edward Sklarz your husband?" the policeman continued.

"Yes."

"May we come in?" asked the second policeman, who had not spoken until this question.

"Yes, of course."

"Please sit down, Mrs. Sklarz," whispered the second policeman.

"Okay."

"We regret to have to inform you that your husband has been killed in a car accident."

"What?" I said.

"Edward Sklarz was killed in a car accident. There appears to have been some alcohol involved. There was a passenger by the name of Sonya Lewis with him. She was also killed. Do you know Sonya Lewis?"

"No, never met her," I answered numbly.

"You will need to go to the morgue later this morning to identify the remains."

With a blank stare, I answered, "Yes, sir."

"Do you want us to call someone to be with you at this time?" asked the second policeman.

"No, I have no one. I will be all right."

I closed the door slowly after the policemen walked through it. I had wanted to be rid of Edward, but not this way.

As I got dressed to go to the morgue, I looked at myself in the mirror. My eyes stared at the face looking back at me. Dare I say that I didn't know what to do—laugh or cry?

LORNA'S SONG

Betty Kossick

Stormy darkness gripped the night. The stand of old oak trees trembled as the wind shook them. If Lorna didn't know better, she'd swear that they'd gathered closer to one another for protection. Even the old Georgia mountain farmhouse shook. Lorna spied Great-great Grandpa's stern-looking photograph swinging, ever so slightly, on the wall. She pushed back the front room curtain. At the same time she tried to gather into her mind the enormity of the turbulence outside, "It's downright scary, isn't it, Ernest? I can't ever recall a wind this bad. Why's it so angry out there?"

Ernest, seemingly unconcerned with the raucous wind, laid down his copy of *The Charlesville Gazette* and beckoned his wife,

"Come sit in the cradle of my arm for a spell, little darlin', and forget your frettin'. It isn't like you, Lorna. You're upset because the boys are comin' home from college in all this commotion, aren't you?"

Not a female to be easily distressed, a hard-scrabble Appalachian woman, Lorna came by her grit honestly, a product of hardy Scotch-Irish descent. She rushed over to Ernest and snuggled close, "You got my number, don't you, husband of mine?"

"Lorna, Lucas, and Micah got themselves level heads, they do. They know the outdoors well enough to take shelter. Those boys of ours got lots of sense."

Then, Ernest broke into a guffaw. "To be honest, sweet love, I haven't been the easiest about this storm, either, but I figure if our boys are gettin' any kind of learnin', they'll know when to take cover. They's smart." Whoosh! C-r-a-ck!

"Well, gal, it sounds like we've lost at least one limb out there." Both of them rushed to check out what happened. Long looks out the big front window showed them more than a downed limb; they spied a split tree. "Meaner than I figured," Ernest admitted.

"I always sorrow to see a downed tree," Lorna lamented. "Trees are so lovely."

Yet within a few minutes after they surveyed the damage, the turbulent wind subsided, and a hush fell outside. Lorna broke into a wide smile, "That's about enough 'weather' for one night. I'm glad it's over with—at least I hope so."

R-i-n-g, r-i-n-g! Ernest hurried to answer the telephone. "Good to hear your voice, Lucas. No problem here, just waitin' for you and your brother to get home. Any problem with you boys? You and your brother OK? No kiddin? A roadblock from a tree! Must be a big one. It is, eh? Sure, don't worry about stayin' over in town. We'll look forward to seein' the two of you in the mornin.' I'm glad the Porters can put you up. But don't put Jackie out for breakfast. Knowin' your Momma, she'll be up by dawn waitin' to put the grits pot on. We've got some plump yeller raisins for it, too. Just what you and Micah like. Sleep good. We got lots of talkin' to do to catch up when you get here."

***

B-e-e-p! Be-e-p! Be-e-p! "They's here, Lorna! They's here! The boys are home."

"Goodness, Ernest, do you think I'm deaf? I heard that car horn a way off. Our sons like to make a big deal of comin' home for all the neighbors to hear. But I like it that they do. It always makes me feel kinda special-like."

"Me too, Lorna. Me too."

"Maw!" Micah yelped as he upped his momma into the air and swung her once around the kitchen. As soon as Micah sat her down, he shouted, "Smell the biscuits, Lucas. It must be like the smell of heaven."

Lucas came over and hugged Lorna so tight that she felt breathless. "You look great, Mom."

"Oh, boys, you're like young bears!" she laughed. The two sons walked to their dad, and the three men embraced in a circle. "Mighty good to see you both. Mighty good!" Ernest exclaimed, with a tight throat. "August to November is a long time not to lay eyes on you."

The three men got into conversation quickly while Lorna sat the breakfast food on the table, "Well, Lucas you're about done at the university now, and Micah, you've got your feet wet for your second year in college. Your Momma's got a big Thanksgivin' dinner planned."

"I can smell it now, Maw!" Micah hollered.

"C'mon, Micah, stop that Maw stuff," Lucas urged. "You're in college now. Call her Mom, or even better, Mother."

"Lucas, he can call me whatever he wants. At home, there's no hi-falutin'," Lorna chastised. Lucas looked down at his bowl of grits and biscuits, "I'm sorry Mom but—"

"O, Maw, Lucas' gotten big-time fancy since he met Lorraine."

"Lorraine?" Lorna inquired.

"I've just grown up, little brother. Lorraine has nothing to do with it."

"Boys, that's enough," Ernest snorted.

"Dad, we really aren't boys any more—even if Micah acts like one."

"I got news for you, young'un, I'll probably be callin' you both boys the rest of your lives. Better get used to it."

"Lucas, you might as well tell Maw and Paw about Christmas while you're acting so high'n' mighty."

"What about Christmas?" Lorna piped in.

"Well, Mom, we can't come home. I promised Lorraine that I'd spend Christmas with her. I've got to have the car to take her home, so that means Micah has to stay at school. I figured that getting home for Thanksgiving would mean lots to you and Dad— but I can't do both. Not now."

"What do you mean—not now?" Ernest snapped.

Micah answered for Lucas, "He's asked her to marry him in June."

"W-ha-t," shouted Ernest and Lorna in unison.

"You're graduatin' in June, son, and we haven't even met this Lorraine person," Lorna almost snarled.

"I know, Mom. I'm sorry about that, but with Lorraine and me both working and going to school, there just hasn't been any time to bring her home to meet you."

"You have no business askin' any girl to marry you. We sent you off to school so you'd do things right. You don't even have a real job yet."

"Yes I do. I've already signed a contract with an engineering company in Richmond. I start July 1. I wanted to surprise you."

"Yep, son, you sure did that!" Ernest retorted.

"But you aren't happy for me—for us—are you?

"I'm truly happy about you landin' a good job, but it surely would be nice to know who you're marryin'. You haven't even shown us a picture of her. Does she have two heads or somethin'? Why didn't you bring her home for Thanksgivin'?" Lorna inquired.

"Her Mom wanted her home. And, Mom, she has one head—a very pretty head. Very."

"Well, ain't that just dandy. When *do* we meet her?" Lorna pouted, slamming a pot in the sink. "An' have you met her folks?"

"Oh, sure, Mom. Been to their home in Richmond three times."

"Three times, eh? But she's not been here once. Isn't that a fine kettle of fish! Stinkin'!" And what about Bonnie? Does she know about you havin' another girl?

"Lucas, I told you Maw would be hot! Look at her red face!" Micah chided with a chuckle.

"Mom and Dad, you'll probably not meet Lorraine until graduation. And as for Bonnie, I'll tell her tomorrow."

"I can't believe what I'm hearin'," Lorna blurted.

"Well this isn't the conversation I expected us to be havin' today, but if Lucas has his mind set—and it looks like he does—we'll just make the best of it," Ernest resolved.

"Make the best of it, you say?!" Lorna spit out the words as she ran into the bedroom, slamming the door shut, causing Great-great Grandpa's picture to swing more than the earlier storm had. The grim look on her face matched the old ancestor's non-smiling portrait.

"Well at least I don't hear Mom bawling," Lucas smiled wryly as he cupped his hand to his ear.

"Give her time. She's too hot to cry right now!" Micah noted.

"Hush it boys. We're needin' to be talkin' sensible like, but let's wait until later. How about the two of you cleanin' up the kitchen? I'll try to calm your Momma."

***

Lorna didn't come out of the bedroom until afternoon. Lucas had driven into town earlier to talk with Bonnie. Micah went to town with Lucas for moral support, he said. However, unknown to Lucas, Micah went more because he'd always been sweet on Bonnie, and he hoped to dry her tears. He figured he'd walk the four miles back home because he knew that Lucas wouldn't hang around. And he didn't want him to.

***

"Mom, are you speaking to me?" Lucas asked Lorna as he stepped into the kitchen to the smell of sweet-potato pies baking.

Lorna was singing a happy tune. Her song rang out like good news to Lucas because he knew his Momma didn't sing without a song in her heart too. She just never equated singing and sorrowing together. Even so, Lorna kept her back to him but kept on singing.

"Mom, I love her. Lorraine is very, very special. She is a Momma's girl, I'll admit that, but she is a good girl. Don't blame her, blame me. I really didn't know how to handle this. She's really is wanting to meet you and Dad. Really. She just doesn't know how to tell her Momma what she wants."

Lorna stopped singing, "Well," she turned, "I've been thinkin', Lucas. Bein' that your daddy can't drive due to his poor eyes, maybe Uncle Bud might be willin' to drive us to the university when winter breaks about March—and before graduation—to meet up with Lorraine. I'll ask Uncle Bud and see what he says.

But I'll tell you right off it will take some doin' because I'm feelin' mighty sorry for Bonnie. I've always counted on her bein' in our family. She's the sweetest thing, and I count her like a daughter. And, tell me, how did she take the news about Lorraine and you?"

"She was a good sport about it. Didn't even cry or anything. I must say I was surprised at that. But then, we weren't even engaged, just sweet on each other."

"Yes, since grade-school days," Lorna reminded him.

"But anyway, she and Micah started talking about the upcoming Christmas parade on Sunday, and they acted like I wasn't even in the room. He said not to wait for him, that he'd walk home. I was really relieved, so I left and stopped by Aunt Lily's for a bit. I told her about Lorraine, and she acted as upset as you. Then I told her how Bonnie accepted it, and she calmed down.

Then, fairly shouting, Lucas said, "That's a great idea, Mom, about Uncle Bud driving you and Dad to meet Lorraine. She'll be so happy." He took his momma's face in his hands and said, "Mom, I know that you'll love Lorraine, too."

Lorna smiled as a tear slipped down to her chin. She wiped it away and another slipped down. Lucas gave his momma one of his tight hugs. She felt comforted by his tenderness.

"By the way, where's Dad?" Lucas asked.

"He went to fetch the rest of the groceries I need for tomorrow's feed."

"What can I do to help you, Mom?"

"Well, I'm wantin' to make some onion pie, too. At least one. I've done enough cryin', so why don't you do the cryin' over the onions? They's always hard on the eyes."

Lorna and Lucas both laughed at the quip. "Fair enough, Mom."

As he peeled and sliced, the tears did come in abundance. About the time Lucas almost felt blinded by them, Ernest walked in. When Dad realized what was what, he burst out in laughter and he, too, said, "Fair enough!" Then, the three of them started laughing together. "What goes around, comes around," Lorna said, with a wink at Lucas.

No sooner had Lucas quit peeling and slicing onions, when Micah walked into the kitchen—holding hands with Bonnie. Lucas' eyes were too tear-filled to notice the hand-holding. But, when Bonnie spied Lucas with weeping eyes, she didn't realize why and rushed over to him. "Lucas, please don't cry. It's all right. Micah and I discovered something today. We realize that we've been very fond of each other for a long time. I didn't want to hurt you by admitting it. Micah didn't want to tell me how he felt because he didn't want to try to take away your girl. When I said I wished you a world of happiness, I really meant it. I'm sure that I'll have a lot of my own, too," she smiled and looked back shyly at beaming Micah.

"So that's why you wanted to go to town with me, Micah, not for the moral support but to move in on Bonnie. You rascal," Lucas said as he hugged his brother. Micah shrugged his shoulders and made a mock sock against Lucas' arm.

Lorna called and motioned for them all to come with her to the front porch. "You see that big split oak? The storm last night did that. I was lookin' out at it when I was poutin' in the bedroom and feelin' powerful sorry for me. I felt like an old split tree. I started studyin' that downed tree, and I got some learnin' from it. I got to thinkin' even that tree, as messed up as it looks, can still be used for things like firewood to keep us warm in winter. Now it's my job to be useful. Lucas is in love with Lorraine, and if he feels anything like I did when I met Ernest, well, then, I'd better be making myself into some good firewood an' make them feel warm at the hearth. An' it looks like there's some other love brewin', so let's put the kettle on an' we'll all have some hot drink to celebrate. I got plenty of dried peppermint leaves, dried from summer's gathering and waitin' for tea-makin'."

Lucas's eyes filled with tears again, but not from onion peeling. As Micah and Bonnie looked into each other's eyes, they, too, brimmed over.

Ernest gulped back his own emotions as he slid his arm around Lorna's waist, just as she started singing again. "Woman, I've loved you since the first day I saw you. You always had a song. We've got a whole lot to be thankful for this Thanksgivin'. As you young'uns can smell, your Mama has a pot of leek soup simmerin'. We can all dive into that with some cornbread, and after feastin' on that, let's all pitch in and get the yummies ready for tomorrow's eatin'."

RACHEL'S DAFFY-DILS

Rose Klix

Liz slammed on the brakes of her white Ford Focus to avoid the red Toyota Highlander's swerving brake lights. The 'Baby on Board' yellow caution signs suction-cupped to the rear window jiggled. Liz thanked God she didn't hit anything, and no one needed her nursing skills.

The young mother opened her door, negotiated the oncoming traffic, and yelled, "Crazy old man. I almost ran over you."

The wind blew the seventyish man's combed-over white strands until they stuck in a spike over their bald home. He pulled up his loose-waist pants with his free hand and tucked-in his brown and tan plaid shirt. Then he resumed waving a handful of daffodils specifically at the SUV. The man turned his blossom weapon on Liz before shooting visual arrows on the neighborhood traffic rubberneckers.

After the lady opened the SUV's back door, she adjusted the car seat while the child cried. Liz's patience waned. She tapped the steering wheel, but avoided the horn button. She fidgeted, but couldn't go around. No shoulder existed on the busy Johnson City, Tennessee, street.

Cars behind Liz honked, and she threw hands overhead. The car radio's digital clock added minutes. The lady shrugged at Liz before starting the engine. They exchanged pleasant nods. The old man continued to wave a fistful of yellow harbingers of spring at the passing traffic.

The incident delayed Liz's daily Home Nurse and Assistance visit to Mrs. Abernathy. The elderly woman resisted shower help. Weekly Meals on Wheels volunteers arrived late. The struggle through bathing tired out her grumpy patient. Liz shook her awake to eat the meager lunch. All day long Liz replayed the morning incident.

"Why would anyone shake daffodils at you?" Liz asked the air.

She was surprised when Mrs. Abernathy answered, "Daffodils? Not until spring."

Two glasses of water helped the patient's stack of medicine pills go down. Liz avoided a discussion of which imagined season camped in the elderly mind. "Be back tomorrow."

"Beans and cornbread?"

"Soup day." Liz wrapped the tie around her wool coat, an insufficient barrier against the chilly air.

Her usual Food City stop could wait. Instead she drove Oakland Street again. *Which house?* She spotted a fieldstone set back from the road. Traffic made it impossible to make a left turn. She remembered the nearby mortuary parking lot, turned in, and stopped the car.

Everything always seems to lead here. She shook off the thought and realized the walk would be treacherous even for half a block.

No alley existed in the neighborhood, which never heard of sidewalks, curbs, and gutters.

Some days Liz wished she could return to Asheville, but she wanted to shake free from the painful memories of nursing her dying husband. Her daughter convinced her she would be better off if they lived within a few miles of each other. The idea sounded good, but as an outside-looking-in prospect.

Loneliness took deep breaths. She wiped at a cheek tear with her shoulder and started the engine.

The next day, the man waved flowers again. He stood where his driveway spilled into the street. The graveled trail disappeared between untrimmed forsythia bushes.

He's going to kill himself. Liz stopped and rolled down her passenger window. Behind her, a pickup driver honked, but she waved him around.

She asked the flower man, "How much?" She smiled as sweet and ineffective as sugar pills.

The old man frowned and held his hand up to his right ear when she repeated.

He shrugged and wrinkled his brow. His whole face froze in a perpetual glare. Liz remembered her grandmother's caution that frowns would freeze into permanent wrinkles.

Liz fumbled through her purse. Another car stopped behind her and honked.

"Hold your horses. Plenty for everyone," the man said.

Flower petals dived to the pavement. Once the oncoming traffic thinned, the car zoomed away. Liz produced a five-dollar bill. Another vehicle squealed to a stop.

"Hothouse ones cost more." He fingered the flowers and counted them. "Okay. Special today." He dropped the whole bouquet on the passenger seat and snatched the money. He showed his hands to the driver behind her. "Missed out." He turned to leave.

"Wait," Liz said.

The man didn't hear her and shuffled through the bushes. More honking continued.

She wanted to circle the block or park at the mortuary. She sighed and looked in the mirror. Liz moved forward. *Why does that old man bug me?* She scratched her chin and glanced down. The bright yellow cheered her into a smile. The radio's digital clock added another minute. *The soup won't fix itself.*

Mrs. Abernathy snatched the bouquet. "Too late for daffodils." She wheezed and pointed. "Reach me that pitcher." She balanced against the sink, poked stems into the water, and hummed.

Vegetable soup bubbled as the onion odor filled the apartment. Liz let her patient nod off during their cribbage game. *I'm not a nurse, but a cook, housekeeper, maid, companion...babysitter.*

Once home, Liz called her daughter. "Suzanne, you've lived here for seven years now. How long before you felt settled?"

"Right away. Friendly people greeted us at church. I love our peaceful neighborhood. Way better than Denver. I'm so glad Billy transferred back here. Call Jackie. You haven't talked to her for a while."

"Long-distance friendships are mythical."

"Met anyone?"

"Mrs. Abernathy."

"I meant a man."

"Not looking. Maybe after I win a NASCAR race."

"Funny." She coughed to cover a giggle. "You miss Daddy."

"Every day." Liz sighed. "He died on my watch."

"Mom, let it go. You hadn't slept in days."

Tears dribbled. Liz wiped them off the phone receiver. "I fell asleep when he needed me." The air held onto a long silent pause.

"I'm cooking for Bill's work buddies tonight. Stop by."

"No, thanks. I wouldn't fit in." Liz cleared her throat to switch subjects. "How's Tyke?"

"Timmy got four As."

"Wow! One in math?"

"No, he still struggles with it."

"Can't help him there." They finished their chat and Liz hung up. She warmed up a bowl of vegetable soup left over from Mrs. Abernathy's. *Perks of the job.*

The next day Liz passed the fieldstone house as slowly as possible. She didn't see him. *Sold enough flowers? Bet he also lives alone.*

After work she parked at the mortuary. Her curiosity outlasted common sense as she walked and dodged traffic. She was glad when she reached the driveway. In the unkempt yard, dandelions and ivy blanketed all the green space meant for grass.

What will I say to him? She tiptoed up the sloping flagstone walkway. While she rehearsed, her insides churned. She jutted out her confident chin.

Liz rapped. No answer. She knocked louder. The curtain on the bay window moved a sliver, but dropped down. Liz surveyed the space. White and pink buds perched on the dogwoods. The redbud trees had finished taking bows. Azaleas promised a hint of color. *Someone loved this property once.* She looked in every direction. *Where are those daffodils?*

"Go away!"

Liz jumped.

"I don't want any magazines, church preaching, nothing." The door slammed behind him. He took two threatening steps towards her.

Liz held up her hands. "Wait—I'm not selling. I'm a nurse."

"Don't need one." He folded his arms.

"I mean, I drive past when I visit my patient."

He looked her up and down. "Nurses don't wear white uniform dresses anymore or those cute little hats."

"No." Liz tugged at the blue weskit blouse over black slacks and pulled her coat closed. "I bought your flowers yesterday. Mrs. Abernathy enjoyed them."

"Rachel's damned daffy-dils."

"Whose?"

"My dead wife."

"She died recently?"

"Four years ago. Her goofy plants bloom soon as that ground-hog's shadow scares them up."

Liz waved around the yard. "Where?"

"Out back. A whole field. She planted more each year."

"You don't like them?"

He turned the doorknob to open the door a crack. "Go away."

Liz cleared her throat. "When my husband died, I took forever to clean out the garage." He stared, but his facial muscles relaxed a little. Liz thought perhaps his skin actually didn't freeze in grue-some folds.

"Joe had assembled a ton of birdhouses and successfully sold them at the church's annual craft fair. He was putting the finish-ing touches on some before he...It took two falls before I got rid of them."

He crossed his hands behind his back and glared at her.

"Several remained in pieces." She shook her head to clear the memory. "I couldn't sell or give away those cut up boards. So I learned how to make birdhouses."

"You?" A smile tickled the corner of his lips. He smoothed his comb-over and tamed the sparse white hairs.

"The Asheville Senior Services introduced me to Ben. He helped me hammer them together. I enjoyed painting different designs."

"They sold at the bazaar?"

Liz nodded. "Went like hotcakes. Joe's regular customers were thrilled they bought 'his' last ones." Her index finger brushed her lips. "Shh. Our secret—and Ben's." She smiled.

"How long now?" He almost whispered.

"Three years. Suzanne thought I'd gone overboard with the birdhouses."

"You did go bonkers."

"What?"

"Me, too." He turned and walked a couple of steps and returned to her. "Sometimes, I wish the crazy patrol would come and lock me up. I could muddle along with some other old coots."

"No friends or family?"

"Who? Where?"

"Suz suggests I visit the senior citizens center here."

"Joining? Too many rules." He waved dismissively.

Liz nodded and shuffled her feet. "She invited me for dinner tonight. Want to go?"

"Strangers? Naw."

"You know me."

"Who are you?"

"Liz."

"I'm Ralph."

Liz reached out her hand. "Nice to meet you, Ralph." Their hands touched for a brief shake.

"Want to pick some of Rachel's daffodils for Suzanne?" Ralph pointed towards the backyard.

"Sure. Then one day I'll show you how to make birdhouses."

"Maybe." He held the door open. Liz wiped her shoes and peeked into a housekeeper's nightmare. Ralph led her through the paper and book maze to look out a back patio window. Liz stared at a yard of sunshine. Yellow and gold daffodil cups smiled and waved in the breeze.

"Beautiful."

"Yeah, but not as pretty as my Rachel." His eyes pooled. He picked up a picture of him helping his wife cut their fiftieth anniversary cake.

"You even have daffodil bouquets on your celebration table."

"They were her wedding flowers. She went crazy over those daffy-dils. Last week would have been our fifty-fifth."

"That's why you wave them at the cars. Daffodils make you sad?"

"More people should enjoy them than just me." Ralph picked up a pair of garden shears. "Let's take your daughter fistfuls of daffy-dils." He smiled at Liz, and she giggled.

THE DAISY FLOWER GARDEN

Jan Howery

Maw Hayley sat on her front porch of her family's 1860s farmhouse, staring out across her front yard at what her mountain neighbors lovingly called 'Maw Hayley's Flower Garden.' Throughout the springtime and summer months, people traveled for miles to visit her half-acre yard that had become known for the beauty of the many colorful flowers in her 'flower garden.'

Flowers from all over the world grew by her hand and her daily hard work. Each week, she would put a few dollars aside from her egg sales to mail order rare and unique flowers. She knew each flower by name, exactly the light or shade it needed and the type of soil it required. All her flowers she nurtured and loved. Blooms of all colors, sizes and shapes swayed and danced in the gentle summer breezes and those light breezes carried the sweet fragrances throughout the farmland for the entire summer. Visitors could smell the perfumed fragrances miles from the farmhouse as they traveled through winding curves of a narrow country dirt road among local cattle farms. They just let their noses lead to them to Maw Hayley's Flower Garden.

My grandmother was called Maw by everyone, even non-family members. She loved being called Maw. She had never met a stranger and always greeted everyone with a smiling hello.

Every summer, she greeted me with that same smile, her loving arms opened wide, and big hugs and kisses. I could not wait until school was out so I could spend those long summer days on the farm with Maw and Paw.

Maw and Paw's life was that of a typical farming family, consumed with raising and milking cows, raising chickens, planting gardens, canning, cooking, and hard work doing all the chores of farm living.

When I arrived for the summer, Paw seemed happy to see me, nicknaming me Daisy, since that was Maw's favorite flower. But most of my time was spent with my grandmother. She taught me many lessons about life, and most of those lessons learned were through the nurturing of her flowers. I loved learning and listening about the different types of flowers and how to appreciate their delicate and precious existence. But most of all, I learned how to recognize the weeds that tried to smother the life from them.

As I was turning eighteen, Maw and I knew that this was going to be my last summer with her and Paw. I was headed to college, and life was changing for me—and for them too. I would no longer be visiting during the summer months. My heading off to college meant that my visits would be short and not as often. So this last summer was very special.

"Daisy, I have a special surprise for you and I just couldn't hardly wait to show ya!" Maw excitedly announced.

"What is it?" I asked with anticipation.

"Well, come with me and I'll show ya. I got 'em last fall and planted them for this season." Maw took my hand and like two young girls, we ran outside to the corner of the yard near the fence. There, cascading along the fence line, were rows and rows of daises. I was startled at the sight. From tall ones to short ones, little ones to big ones, and like wildflowers, all were bursting with colors of yellow, pink, white, and purple, hues of blues, oranges, and more colors than I could imagine.

"Maw—how on earth did you do this?" I asked, knowing that there was no explanation needed.

"I just wanted you have a corner of my world like the way you'll always have a corner in my world and my heart, no matter where you are." Maw cried, her voice breaking on each word.

Her tears streamed down her face, and for the first time in my life, I realized that Maw was not a young woman. Lines of life had left their footprints of both happy times and sad times on her face. Her smile was weak and was lined with a deep sadness that only time could mark. I saw my grandmother age before my eyes.

"Maw, I will be back. I promise," I declared as tears filled my eyes.

"Well, now, we don't need to be watering these daisies with our tears. Too salty for 'em. And we got chores we gotta get to."

With hugs and kisses, I put on my best smile and asked, "Where to Maw?"

"The creeping phlox is being swallower'd up by those running weeds. They're just suckin' the life out of 'em." Maw said.

"We had that problem last year, Maw. I thought that we killed them out."

"It's the root. We gotta get to the root of the problem. Like they say, bad to the core. And weeds are bad to the root. Just like people."

"Like people? How so?" I asked with a quirky giggle.

"People rooted in kindness and doin' good will surely have goodness in their lives. But those without good roots, their deeds are bad," Maw said with meaningful conviction.

"Is there ever a chance for them? What if they never take good root?" I asked with a little smirk grin.

"Daisy, honey, of course. But some people have no roots. But it is worse to have bad roots, and just like weeds, they can last a lifetime. Those without roots, well, what happens is that they just wither and die. You know that you gotta look at the roots. And you know you gotta plant good seeds, 'cause if they ain't got good roots, they ain't gonna grow up right. And those with bad roots, they gotta turn 'round or die. And weeds are everywhere—only those with strong good roots will survive among the weeds, 'cause those weeds got roots, too."

"Now Maw, just how could these running weeds with bad roots do good?" I asked with a smile.

"Running weeds have their place somewhere, just not in with my creeping phlox!" Maw said as she pulled a handful of weeds from the ground with dirt and roots and tossed them in the air.

That summer went by quickly. Paw worked every day, except on Sunday, in the fields as usual. Maw and I enjoyed every morning checking on the grove of daisies. She called it her 'Darling Daisies' garden. Maybe because of the tremendous variety of daisies, it seemed that this summer more visitors than ever stopped by to view her flower garden. Like always, if asked, Maw would give them a starter of any flower or plant with instructions on how to care for it.

"Don't water too much, don't give 'em too much light, give 'em lots of light, and water 'em every day" were words that I must have repeated in my sleep. Words to live by, as Maw would say. "Flowers and life are the same—too much or not enough will kill it."

As I packed my suitcase on my last morning of my summer vacation, I looked out the window for the last time. The sky was overcast with cloudiness and dreariness. Guess it was sad, too. Even the flowers seem to be sagging and drooping in sadness. I walked down to the kitchen where and Paw was looking at Maw with a puzzled frowned on his face.

I could see the worry in his face. "What's wrong Paw?" I asked, glancing over to Maw.

Before Paw could answer, Maw whipped around and said, "There ain't nothing wrong. I just got a little confused for a minute—I'm all right now. Just need that second cup of coffee to get goin'. Miss Daisy, are you ready to go out and cheer up our Darling Daisies? They seem awful sad this morning, and..."

Maw stopped in the middle of her sentence, and her facial expression drifted into the distance. She lost all expression, and her face became blank. Paw continued to look at her and then he looked to me with an unspoken worry. Was Maw choked up over my leaving? I sure was. I was near tears. Suddenly, Maw jumped up and said, "Well, aren't we goin' to visit those crying daisies?"

Paw smiled and nodded. Maw and I walked out to the Darling Daisies garden, sipping our coffee and talking about the how quickly the summer had passed, when Maw said, "Daisy, you're my world, and I love you. You've been like a daughter to me, and when your Mother and Dad were killed in that car accident, I didn't think that I could go on. I was such a mess. Out of my eight children, my son, Curtis—God bless 'em—he took you to raise. I couldn't have survived my loss without you. I'm gonna miss you, and I want you to take care of yourself. And remember

flowers and life are the same—too much...or not enough...and...
and...be a good root," she said struggling to say her words.

Her words seemed a little jumbled, and I could not get past
the deep sadness in her eyes. I could no longer hold back my
tears. At that moment, I knew that it was not just my life that
was changing, but Maw's, too. Her garden was her reason for
living. I was her root in her garden.

Working through college and keeping up my class assign-
ments, I did not have time to visit during my four years at college.
Many times when I called to speak to Maw and Paw, Maw was
usually too busy to come to the phone. Paw would say that he
would tell her that I called, and she missed me. My last message I
left with Paw was, "I will be there right after my graduation next
week. My bags are packed, and I will be home for the summer.
I can't wait." I noticed that Paw did not seem overjoyed, but I
knew he and Maw would be glad to see me.

I walked across the stage, was handed my diploma. I walked,
or really ran, straight to my car. I was on the road with a mission
to see that farmhouse and stroll through that never-ending flower
garden. All were vivid in my heart and mind.

* * *

*Maw sat on her front porch of their family's 1860s farmhouse,
staring out across her front yard to what her mountain neighbors lovingly
called 'Maw Hayley's Flower Garden.'*

"I think that it's time," Paw said quietly.

Maw stared with an expressionless blank face. Her hair has
grown so gray and the sparkle in her eyes was gone.

I placed a daisy from her Darling Daisies garden in her lifeless hand. As the nurse turned to push her wheelchair down the
ramp off the porch, just for a moment, Maw's face glowed as she
looked down at the daisy in her hand. With a soft gentleness in

her voice and a sudden sparkle in her eyes, she turned, looked at me and quietly spoke, "My darling Daisy, root of all that is good."

Three months later, as Maw's coffin was closed, I gave her a kiss goodbye and placed her favorite flower in her hand—a daisy.

THE MIDWIFE OF WETZEL COUNTY

Carolina Major Diaz San Francisco

When I met Edna Dale Fouty, I became a daughter of the mountains. This is how it happened:

It was a cool night in the early spring of 1938 when I arrived to Earnshaw Town, West Virginia, to visit Edna, but I didn't find her at home. She was at the Astons' instead, which her husband and children told me was across town but not far away. While I was waiting for her and being served dinner, I looked up with incredible curiosity. She was listening to the heartbeats of young Jane Lee

Aston's unborn child inside a rustic bedroom that was dimly lit, with the watchful mountains outside.

Edna, an expert in midwifery, or 'life itself' as she called the job, comforted sweaty Jane Lee Aston with rubbings, calming oils, and sweet songs as she feared the pain coming with birth.

"A precious child of our mountains is about to be born," Edna sang softly and beautifully like she always did in her church, with a plentiful faith in the sacred verses of the purity of the soul she knew by heart so well.

She brought Jane Lee warmth and peace, as well as water to drink, while Mary Alice, the grandmother to be, stood still by the wretched wooden door, observing the midwife of Wetzel County preparing her offspring to come into their world. For her, Edna Dale Fouty was the greatest in those fragile moments. She was the woman who everyone in Earnshaw Town, and as far as Hundred Town, loved to greet with a "Good morning, Mrs. Fouty!" and "Good evening, Mrs. Fouty!"

"Contractions will continue now. Call the doctor early tomorrow morning," Edna commanded to Mary Alice as she washed her hands, "And send the boy for me, I will help. Our mountains are watching. A child is going to be born soon."

I impatiently waited for Edna at her home, sitting at her kitchen table, surrounded by her young children—James, Roy, Ray, and Ruby—who asked endless questions regarding who I was, where I came from, why I was there. They did all this while reaching and touching my precious scarlet hat. I was certain that I was giving the patriarch Benjamin Franklin Fouty an amusing time. By the time I tried to grow comfortable, Edna was on her way with Charles Fouty, her teenage son whom Edna had named as her guardian, since he considered himself a man. I later learned that Charles Fouty, a red-haired boy, always escorted his mother. He was proud that his mother had assisted in more than sixty births and that she and the babies frequently arrived before the doctor.

The front door opened at the moment I least expected. I was feeling admired and reverenced as I blinked playfully and was telling the family in a very fantastic way about where in I lived in New York City, when I saw Edna enter the house and take off her shoes in a preoccupied manner. My eccentric mood vanished when I laid eyes on her, a woman who was about my own age. My cousin. She was tall, thin, and fair, as well as something else that I couldn't put my finger on.

"You're back," Benjamin Franklin stood, ready to go. "You have a visitor, Meredith Coleman. She says your Aunt Grace sent her."

"Mother, she comes from New York City!" Ruby exclaimed.

"Good evening, Mrs. Fouty," I hailed, leaving the table and graciously going toward her. "I didn't mean to come unexpectedly. Aunty Grace insisted. She said I should see you before my leave."

I was very attractive, more than ever, and I wanted Edna, everyone really, to notice such a new splendor. I felt her gaze upon my dress, my hair, and my fine boots. I saw her radiating enchantment for a moment that seemed like an eternity. I assumed she strived to recognize me, but I have been long away.

"Meredith Coleman! No, this ain't you!" Edna shouted.

We drew closer to one another and embraced like two strangers. Benjamin left, and Edna ordered all her children to follow and to leave us alone. Edna asked me to sit down again and she took a seat next to me. She enquired about my family, all of whom were living further south in Coburn Town, about the length of my stay, and about my life. So I started all over again, feeling flamboyant and like an achiever, doing all the talking and making all the funny remarks, while she smiled and assented with, "Really?" and "Wow!"

I told Edna about the great city, the temples of fashion, shops, theaters, people from all over the world. I became fond of her because she marveled at my telling. I secretly thought I was fortunate because I had left, and that I should save her from the arduous life of the mountains, and take her with me to help her to free herself and became somehow like me: a successful, modern, and independent woman. As I thought this, she kept asking and wondering about all this other world I knew beyond her mountains and what it was like. There came a time when I just couldn't go on. She started to shine with enjoyment at the taste of a little adventure and her delightful openness to me.

I supposed it was my turn to ask questions, since it was the proper thing to do. So I did, first searching for clues about her, because I knew little or nothing about her. I glimpsed at her face which was clean and honest; at her hair which was wild and fair; at her eyes which were tiny and bright; and then over the room, which had honey-colored boards for walls. I admired her children—they were my first thought. I said they were beautiful and polite, but there was this silence between us and around. I became quiet. Edna looked peaceful and reached for my hands. I found hers to be large and in touch with the earth. Mine were smaller, softer, and finely manicured.

"My children are my blessings, and they are all grown now," she finally said with a deep and serene voice, paced with words that breathed at their end, "and I pray to our Lord and praise our mountains for all of us."

She was sweet. She gently released my hands and rose to go about the kitchen, tidying up and turning down the lights of some lamps. The room grew darker.

"Here in the mountains," she started, "we are privileged. We have so much. I don't know where to start, pretty flower. Well, Benjamin is a hard worker. He goes out of town sometimes. We keep pigs most winters. I grow a garden. I bake bread and pies with our pumpkins. Sometimes I bring them to church and give them as gifts to the unfortunate or to some needy family. We have a good town, I believe."

Edna called me 'pretty flower' in an appealing tone, and I was flattered. I discovered that she, too, could be fancy in her ways. She returned to the chair and sat by my side. I sensed her contentment and perhaps, happiness at having me there.

"And we have our songs, Meredith. Songs you have never heard, songs you would never forget." She went on, "I sing when it rains and when it is sunny. I sing all the same. I like to think of new ones for our Sundays in church."

Edna carried on, telling me about divine lyrics and the old piano sitting in her in church, amazing me until I asked her to sing for me. She laughed, and she said she would sing another time because everything in the hollows at that moment was waiting for us to seal our mouths and go to sleep. That night ended just like that. She led me into a bedroom where her daughter was sound asleep, and she blessed me with a kiss.

I don't recall how I slept, but I clearly remember the next day well. How can I forget! I opened my eyes inside that unfamiliar room, noticing resin fumes and the thick aromas of coffee and pumpkin pie coming from the kitchen. When I realized where I was, I became aware of my looks and my hair. I tried to groom myself as best I could. There was no one home and I went outside. The breeze met me first, then the brightness of the morning light, and then the scene painted green. I could see below the hollows in the distance, downtown, two centenary churches, and up ahead of me the great mountains with their hickories, pines and old oaks, and their mysteries.

"Edna!" I shouted.

I stumbled uphill, watching my steps because I hardly ever wandered on dirt or gave myself way among tall, wild weeds and pinchy bushes. I grabbed my dress and endured up through the denseness of all shades of green, watching the birds' flights and listening to their songs, until the black of Edna's gown appeared in my view.

"Edna?"

She did not turn, but continued, on bended knees, working with her arms and hands as she dug in what appeared to be a rather marvelous garden re-emerging again, with lively sprouts with the winter slowly moved away. I had needed to touch her shoulder since she had not heard me calling or noticed my presence.

"Meredith!" She didn't seem surprised. "This is my garden. How do you like it? I have my herbs here. Bloodroot and dandelions grow free on that end, and our vegetables grow over there. See? It's their time to blossom. Come closer. They won't bite you!"

I hesitated before kneeling because I didn't know how hard the soil would feel. Our elbows met as I moved closer to look at that magic of birth and growth there in the skins of Edna's mountains; seeing her gently touching the new leaves to show me, I felt her mysticism being revealed.

Suddenly, the voice of the young Charles Fouty reached to us like an arrow rapidly flying between the trees.

"Mother! It's coming! It's time! It's the Astons!"

I spotted the boy running uphill and jumping over all the bushes like a deer.

"It's coming! The baby is coming, Mother!" he kept shouting.

Edna left my side rather fast and went down to the house, so I ran after her with trembling feet.

"Has the doctor been called?" I heard Edna asking her son.

"Yes, Mother. Hurry!"

At the house, Edna washed her hands and hurried.

"You're coming with us," she said.

I wanted to know where exactly we were going because I needed to decide, but Edna was already heading down the hill with her guardian, all the way to the Astons' through the shortcuts in the woods. I had to follow. What else was I going to do? I rambled behind them, a little scornful at her for being demanding, while I quietly observed her stride and her strong back. I believed Edna Dale Fouty had bewitched me.

A local farming couple crossed our way and greeted with a "Good morning, Mrs. Fouty!" and stopped to watch us as we moved along the path. After the crossing, and after reaching an isolated clearing, we found the house of the Astons' and the ongoing fuss inside. I saw Edna enter and disappear into the darkness through the door, and Charles go to a corner in the porch where he sat. With every step toward the house, I could hear the sounds from Jane Lee. Louder and louder, Jane Lee screaming was soft at times, terrified and agonizing at other times. At the door, in between the outside and the unknown, I debated whether I should enter or not. This went on until Mary Alice came and fetched me, urgently asking me to bring warm water from the stove and clean bedroom towels.

"Push, Jane! Push!" I heard Edna exclaim.

The house wasn't big. With blurred vision I searched for my way, feeling like a novice as I ingested all of the roars and yells. When I found the hot pot and the towels, I promptly brought them into the bedroom. At the same moment that I entered, Jane Lee finally pushed the hardest and the longest, which was exactly as Edna had asked her to do. I dropped the pots and towels on the floor at the corner of the bed. I watched as Mary Alice held her daughter's hands to give her strength. Then I saw the tiny head showing.

"One more push, Jane! One more push!" Edna said, while holding one of Jane's thighs with one hand, and the top of the baby's head with the other.

Jane complained she could push no more.

"Jane, you are going to breathe now. Breathe, Jane! Now, push! One more push! One more!" Edna kept encouraging.

And then the miracle occurred in front of my eyes. Jane pushed once more, and the child emerged entirely into our world and was born. I heard the cry, the joy of Mary Alice, and Edna praying and singing, "A child of our mountains is born."

On that day I became a daughter of the mountains that have always watched me. I had not known it until that moment I shared with Edna at the Astons'. I travelled back to New York City, and I longed for my return to Wetzel County like never before.

***

In memory of Edna Dale Fouty (1908-1982),
mother of Ruby J Mclain, Ray A Fouty, and Roy Lee Fouty,
and paternal grandmother of my mother-in-law, Kristine Major

ABOUT THE AUTHORS

Rachel Burdine is a native of Kingsport, Tennessee, and teaches fifth grade in the Sullivan County school district. She is a 2004 graduate of East Tennessee State University and received her Master's from Union University in 2008. Her five-year-old son, Bo, keeps her busy. Rachel recently rediscovered her love of horses and four-wheelers, much to Bo's delight, and neither of them can get enough riding time to suit them! Rachel and Bo attend Beulah Baptist Church.

Lori C Byington resides in Bristol, Tennessee, with her husband, Mark, and son, Lee. The family loves to snow ski, hunt, and be on the lake. They are members of the Team Beech Ski Team, which is based at Beech Mountain, NC. Lori also owns a registered Quarter Horse. She is a graduate of King College (BA, English) and East Tennessee State University (MA, English) and has taught English, including college-level courses in composition and literature, since 1986. Lori loves to write and compose poetry mainly, but she dabbles in short stories also.

The daughter and granddaughter of coal miners, **Rebecca D Elswick** lives in the coalfields of Appalachia. She and her husband have three children and—at last count—five dogs. Rebecca has a Master's in Education from East Tennessee State University and teaches English and creative writing. Her short fiction has received numerous awards and has appeared in journals and magazines. *Mama's Shoes*, her award-winning debut novel, was published by Writer's Digest. Visit Rebecca's website (rebeccaelswick.com).

Lisa Hall and her husband reside in Fall Branch, Tennessee, with their two little girls and an English bulldog. Aside from writing, public speaking, and conducting workshops, Lisa stays busy taking her daughters to their sports, guitar lessons, school activities, and play dates. Lisa is the author of the *Cutie Pies Chronicles* series and *Burton the Sneezing Cow*. *Alice Pemberton's Orchard* is Lisa's fifth published short story. Catch Lisa on her website (lisahallauthor.com) or at Fans of the *Cutie Pies Chronicles* on Facebook.

April Hensley's favorite memories of childhood are of exploring the woods, wildlife, creeks, and rivers of the Appalachian Mountains. Now she spends much of her free time outdoors gardening, hiking, boating, and enjoying nature. April was published in *Self-Rising Flowers*, writing as Maggie Thomas. Recently she had a short story published in *Inlightenment* e-magazine. April lives in northeastern Tennessee with her husband (and best friend) Danny and their beloved fur-babies.

Linda Hudson Hoagland of Tazewell, Virginia, is a graduate of Southwest Virginia Community College and has won acclaim for her 9 mystery novels. In addition, Linda has written 6 nonfiction books, released a collection of prize-winning short writings, and produced a collection of poems. She is a retired public-school employee and the mother of 2 sons. Currently Linda is serving on the Advisory Board for the Humanities Degree Program of Bluefield State College and as Vice President of the Appalachian Authors Guild and Associates. You can contact Linda at lhhoagland@yahoo.com.

Lynda A Holmes began writing at the age of 12, when she won a contest for her essay about a trip to Washington DC and New York.

She is a retired teacher whose publications include professional articles, short stories, memoirs, poems, a children's book, historical articles for *The Gainesville Times* newspaper, and award-winning plays. Lynda has received a Women in the Arts Recognition Award in literature and drama authorship from the Daughters of the American Revolution.

Born in rural Southwestern Virginia, **Jan Howery** lives her life by the Appalachian precept of the importance of spiritual faith, family roots, and a strong work ethic. Jan is a world traveler, public speaker, local theater actress, mistress of ceremonies, and business owner. Her specialized training includes a BS in Psychology, postgraduate training in marriage counseling, and certification as a hypnotist. Now residing in Tennessee, Jan is a contributing writer for *Voice Magazine for Women*. Jan's love of writing shines through the details of childhood farm-living in rural Appalachia in her heart-touching story *The Daisy Flower Garden*.

Pam Keaton is the author of three published short stories, *Road Trip to Albany*, *The Baker's Cabinet*, and *Fried Okra*. In addition to creating the cover art for close to a dozen books, Pam illustrated Lisa Hall's recent book, *Burton the Sneezing Cow*. Most notably, Pam is the author-illustrator of *Malina and the Lost Art*, a novel for middle-schoolers, and she currently is working on a sequel. Visit www.pamkeaton.com for more information.

Rose Klix is an award-winning and published author and poet and a produced playwright. She enjoyed living near the Appalachian Mountains, but she recently decided to return to the Black Hills of South Dakota, where she grew up. Check out Rose's website (RoseKlix.com).

Betty Kossick solo-authored *Beyond the Locked Door* (2006) and *Heart Ballads* (2009, Little Creek Books), both of which are available on amazon.com. In addition, Betty has contributed to 59 other books, including several for Mountain Girl Press, and she's looking forward to several more publications during 2014. Betty has been a busy writer–journalist–poet for 43 years, and she continues to freelance. Betty's motto: Joy in Jesus. Feel free to email her at bkwrites4u@ hotmail.com.

Gretchen McCroskey grew up on a farm near Abingdon, Virginia, where she enjoyed listening to stories told by older relatives and neighbors, as she captured the cadence of expressions to be crafted into lines of poetry and prose. A graduate of King University and Hollins University, Gretchen retired as Associate Professor of English at Northeast State Community College in 2011. She is the author of *Finding My Way Home*, a poetry chapbook published in 2009.

Carolina Major Diaz San Francisco lives in Rhode Island with her husband, Tobias, and cats, Angel and Canela. She works as a pharmacy dispenser at the Rhode Island Hospital and researches healthcare systems and health-seeking behavior in Rhode Island and the Boston area. Currently Carolina is preparing her research project on traditional medicine in Equatorial Guinea, West Africa. She has published the novel *Mi Madre Es Una Estrella* and the children's book *The Fantastic Herbs*.

A Chattanooga native with strong north-Georgia roots, **Janie Dempsey Watts** writes both fiction and nonfiction stories. Her novel *Moon Over Taylor's Ridge* earned Janie nominations for Georgia Author of the Year and a Southern Independent Bookseller Award and was a finalist in the Augusta Literary Festival. Janie lives near the family farm in Georgia and writes with her American bulldog, Bella, at her feet. Please visit her at janiewatts.com.

**Jan-Carol
Publishing, Inc**

"every story needs a book"

**LITTLE CREEK BOOKS
MOUNTAIN GIRL PRESS
EXPRESS EDITIONS
DIGISTYLE
ROSEHEART PUBLISHING**

JANCAROLPUBLISHING.COM